Everything is Going to Be Okay

Samantha Baldwin

Dedication

To L & D

But when anything is exposed by the light it becomes visible
Ephesians 5:13.

Prologue

I woke up one morning with a little tap, tap, tapping sound at the door. My heart jumped. Lewis shouted from the lounge, "Mummy, what's that noise?"

Cautiously, I climbed out of bed and tiptoed through the hallway, stopping at the pane of frosted glass. Spotting the distinct shape of a pheasant hitting our window with its beak, I was filled with relief.

'Only a beautiful bird come to say, "Good Morning",' I tell the boys.

Rubbing my eyes and walking into the large, open plan kitchen/sitting room, I planted a kiss on both my sons' heads.

'Hi, Mummy,' they said in unison, not lifting their eyes from the screen. They were sitting together on one of two large comfy sofas that dominated the homely space, pyjamas on, knees up to their chests, playing their iPads, completely oblivious to the danger we were all in.

Staring from one to the other, I thought my heart might burst with love. My babies, my everything. There was nothing I wouldn't do for my sons. Lewis was nine, then, a few months from his tenth birthday. "I'll soon be double digits," he had been saying repeatedly, for months. And little Daniel had just turned six. He still had his baby face. They were such handsome boys, both tall for their ages. Lewis with his beautiful aqua coloured eyes and smile that could light up a room. And sweet little Daniel, with his large dark brown doe-eyes.

'Who want's hot chocolate?' I asked, careful to keep my voice light and upbeat.

'Me!' Lewis cried.

'And me!' his little brother chipped in.

Flicking the switch on the kettle I set about preparing a drink for the boys and a peppermint tea for myself. I tried to manage a few morsels of the breakfast I was cooking, but it was futile. My appetite had completely disappeared. The chocolate and peppermint filled my nostrils with their pungent scent, but still I didn't crave food. Perhaps it was the intense anxiety? Perhaps it was the lack of nutrients? But my senses were acutely sharp, like an animal in the wild.

After breakfast Daniel went in search of his clothes. Lewis and I were content to lounge around in our pyjamas, but not the little one. He liked being dressed and the independence of choosing what he'd wear, even though it was always jogging bottoms and a top with a cartoon logo. To prove my point, he came sauntering into the room with a "Fireman Sam" t-shirt.

'I want a cape, Mummy,' he exclaimed, darting around the room with his plastic sword. 'A red one.'

'He could use one of his cloths, Mummy,' Lewis suggested. 'We can dye it red.'

Daniel slept with a white muslin cloth, every night. He'd done so, since he was a baby.

'Let's do it!' I enthused.

All three of us set about changing the colour of the cloth with red felt pens. It took a while, but Daniel was delighted with the result.

'Look at me, I'm Superman!' He laughed, climbing under and over the little table, his newly dyed cape swinging behind him.

I turned on the TV, keen to distract my mind from the avalanche of thoughts waiting to engulf it.

'That's me!' Lewis shrieked. 'Mummy, Daniel, look, we're on the TV.'

I grabbed the remote control and hit the 'off' switch. Daniel stared at the empty screen, his mouth wide open.

'Boys,' I said, pulling them both close. 'There's something Mummy's got to tell you…'

It was eleven am on day ten and food supplies were running low. We were left with potatoes, some vegetables, rice, pasta, maple syrup, flour and milk. We had run out of chocolate, bread, cheese, peanuts – everything the boys liked. There were no snacks now. We had four more days here before I would have to decide our next move. I stood in the kitchen chopping peppers for a stir fry.

The task was interrupted by a quiet knock on the outside door. My body stiffened. Hardly daring to breath, I crept across the living space and whispered for the boys to come with me into the en-suite bathroom of my bedroom. Once there, we sat huddled on the tiled floor and listened. I prayed out loud for us to be kept safe.

'Please God, don't let them find us.'

The knocking stopped. We could hear voices outside. It sounded like a couple of women talking. And then the voices stopped. Breathing out, we remained in the bathroom, until we were certain we were once again alone.

An e-mail pinged on the computer. The staff required

access to change sheets and towels.

'We don't need fresh sheets. We are leaving in a few days,' I replied, anxious to veto any more visits from staff. Immediately afterwards, I began to panic. *Would that be suspicious?*

The luxury lodge was very comfortable. It was cosy and warm, had everything we needed and more besides, including heated wooden floors and double-glazed windows. I had my own en-suite bedroom with a four-poster bed. The boys shared a room with a single bed on either side. They also had their own bathroom. In different circumstances, it might have been the destination of a lifetime.

The outside of the small house had a large terrace, complete with a hot tub, pine furniture and a spectacular view of the wood. We had only used the hot tub once. After that, I realised it wasn't safe. The breath-taking views were also wasted as we had to keep the blinds down at all times. There were too many other lodges dotted around; we couldn't afford to be seen.

I made the guys a meagre lunch and coaxed them into eating it, with promises of feasts when we next got to the shops. As they returned to their consoles, I retreated to the worktop in the small kitchen area. Opening my laptop, I braced myself for what I might read.

Over the past week I had morphed from an average single mother and homemaker, without so much as a parking ticket to my name, into a wanted fugitive. My face stared back at me from a dozen major news outlet websites. There was a photo of us on the BBC home page. They making out I was a threat to the boys. Me! As if I could harm a hair on their heads. Adjectives like "dangerous" and "psychotic" were flung about and wild allegations were presented as fact. My head pounded as I switched from headline to headline, desperately aware how powerless I was to refute any of the lies they were printing. It's not like I could call them up and say, "This is what actually happened…"

The police had released a plea for me to return. The officer they'd enlisted for the job spoke directly to the camera, in a quiet, reassuring voice.

"We promise you if you come back, we will treat you fairly,' she said. 'We can't imagine how scared you must be, and we are here to reassure you that you will be listened to, if you hand yourself in.'

Listened to? They'd had years to listen to us and refused. It seemed highly implausible they would listen to us now.

'We need to know the children are safe,' the gentle voice continued.

And just like that, I knew they were lying. They knew my children were safe with me. Of that fact, they were absolutely certain.

In contrast to my media portrayal as some kind of deranged, scorned woman, social media perceived me more open-mindedly. There was a staggering amount of support for me on Facebook and Twitter. It was overwhelming to think organically the truth was spreading. A petition was doing the rounds and had clocked up thousands of supporters. Friends had even set up a "Just Giving" page, and many people donated in the hope they could pay for the legal support we so clearly needed. A stray tear trickled down my cheek.

'What's up, Mummy? What is it?' My eldest was hyper vigilant and noticed the slightest thing.

'Loads of people believe us and know that I am telling the truth. They have raised lots of money for us.'

'Really?' Lewis's eyes widened. 'How much?'

'Thousands,' I replied.

'Thousands!' Lewis repeated. 'That is lots, that's bound to help us, won't it, Mummy?'

'I should think so,' I replied, ruffling his hair.

I didn't say I had already spent tens of thousands, and it hadn't helped at all.

***

As the afternoon wore on, I kept the boys' spirits up playing hide and seek and doing my best impression of Superman. Lewis suggested a game of 'I spy'. Flopping on the four-poster bed, he began, 'I spy with my little eye something beginning with "H".'

'Helicopter?' ventured Daniel.

'No,' Lewis replied.

It wasn't a bad guess as we'd heard them overhead, several days. My keeping it together- self figured it must be some kind of training exercise happening locally. But a part of me wondered. The papers were saying that a hundred team task force had been set up to find us. If they could justify that level of resources to locate an unarmed woman with no history of mental ill health or violence, then anything seemed possible.

'You guess now, Mummy.' Lewis's words brought me back to the present.

'Hand?' I suggested, struggling to see any "H" words in the room.

'Hulk?' Daniel interrupted, unable to contain his joy at having figured it out.

Eventually the game came around to "B".

'Bum!' Daniel shouted, and Lewis snorted with laughter.

The three of us rolled around the mattress giggling, with the boys intermittently calling out "Bum".

***

As afternoon gave way to early evening the three of nestled

together on the couch to watch the Channel 5 Movie. It was a true story about a mother and daughter who had been separated for twenty-five years as someone pretending to be a nurse had stolen the daughter from the hospital when she was a newborn.

'I'm bored!' Daniel declared ten minutes in, and went in search of a less sedentary pass time. Lewis, in contrast, had his eyes glued to the screen. For him, the idea of corrupt adults and vulnerable babies was all too real.

'What if the police get us, Mummy?' he asked, when his little brother was out of earshot.

'Don't worry, they won't. Mummy's gonna protect you.' I squeezed his hand.

'Why can't you protect us at home?' Lewis squeezed back so hard I thought my fingers would break.

'Because, darling, the police would find us there.'

Stray hairs were dangling in front of his barely blue eyes, so I carefully brushed them away.

'Why don't they believe us, Mummy?' He looked at me earnestly.

'I don't know, sweetheart,' I replied, pulling him close.

It wasn't strictly the truth. Though I'd been on the run for less than a fortnight, I was learning, quickly, how things really worked. I was a wanted woman. My children were wards of the state. Our local police force had invested half the year's budget in tracking us down. To me, the question was no longer, "Why don't they believe us?". It was, "Who the hell are they protecting?"

After the movie, the boys amused themselves whilst I assembled some of the remaining ingredients into a dinner. Though decidedly unappealing, they made a decent job of eating it, reminding me, once again, what troopers they were.

I washed up while Lewis and Daniel played on their

iPads. I gave them about an hour before calling bedtime. I'd managed to keep some semblance of routine in our otherwise chaotic environment, and the boys took it in turns to shower, whilst I readied their room for the night.

At about 8:30pm, I climbed into Daniel's bed with him, wrapping my arms around him and snuggling in, as I read to him. Tonight, he chose one of his favourite books *That Pesky Rat* about a homeless street rat. After I finished the story, he settled into bed, getting hold of his 'cloth' and his grey kitten.

'I love you so much, Daniel.'

He looked up at me with his large brown sleepy eyes. 'I love you so much too, Mummy' he replied.

I kissed his soft round cheek and inhaled the smell of his freshly washed hair. I gave his face one last stroke before tip-toeing out of the bedroom and into the lounge, where Lewis was still playing on his iPad.

'Right, Lewis, time for bed now, sweetheart.' I bent down to him.

'Okay, Mummy, just one more minute.'

'One.' I held my hand up and feigned a stern face.

Lewis smiled.

A couple of minutes later Lewis came into my room and crawled into my bed.

'Not until your teeth are brushed,' I told him, lifting the duvet gently, so he could slide out and into my bathroom. I had the book we were reading open, ready for his return. It was about horses. Lewis loved them. I shut the book slowly after finishing a chapter.

'Right, Lewis, time for bed.' I placed the book on my bedside table.

'Can't I sleep in here tonight, Mummy?' he asked, smiling at me.

'No,' I answered, smiling back. 'You can sleep in your

own room with Daniel.' I playfully pulled him by the legs from one side of the bed to the other. He was getting so big. He shrieked with laughter.

'Come on, Lewis, in your own bed.' I took him into his room, and we hugged, and I kissed him on his cheek.

'Goodnight,' I whispered.

He had such beautiful soft skin. I stood in the doorway, the hall light illumining my sleeping children. My big, brave Lewis. He had come on leaps and bounds since the days when he was too terrified to sleep without me. Somehow, I had managed to get him to share a room with Daniel, but it was a recent development. *Would this craziness derail all his progress?*

Little Daniel turned in his bed and gave out a little snore. He looked so content and at peace with the world.

'Mummy's gonna keep you both safe,' I told my dreaming boys. It sounded more plausible when I said it out loud.

***

That evening, I made a pancake mixture for breakfast. I had to put lots of chia seeds in. That would make it more substantial, and there would be enough for the day after too. The boys wouldn't mind as long as they had plenty of maple syrup.

Our rations meant I was barely eating, but I had no appetite and hardly noticed. I could see I had lost lots of weight, the way my clothes hung off my skeletal frame. *'The Fugitive Diet,'* I thought, wryly. *Almost no solid food and lots of startled jumps to the window and rolls to the ground…just in case.*

I flipped over my laptop and took a quick inventory of where they were with the search. I skim read a few paragraphs on the local police website, before slamming it shut. They were expanding the parameters to include holiday homes and caravan parks. The net was closing in.

I fell to my knees and prayed.

∗∗∗

It was one am, when they drilled through the door and smashed through the glass. I was wrenched out of sleep with deafeningly loud noises. I leapt out of bed with lightning speed as the terrifying reality set in. My heart racing, I ran into my sons' bedroom. Lewis was sat up in bed screaming loudly. I ran over to him, and together we sat on his bed as he gripped onto me with all his might. Daniel was still in his bed.

'I love you boys!' I shouted.

'Daniel, Daniel, Come here!' I was desperate to hold them both. He was silent, across from us. I yearned to grab him but dared not leave his brother.

'I love you,' I screamed as eight armed police officers burst in.

'Get off him!' a policeman yelled.

But how could I tear myself away from my beautiful son? Two more officers yanked me from his arms. Lewis's screams filled the air as I was shoved outside into the cold dark night, in nothing but my pyjamas. A female officer held me on one side, a male officer held the other.

'Mummy!' Lewis howled.

'I want my mummy,' Daniel yelled.

They handed me my wellies because I was standing bare foot in the glass they'd broke, to gain access to the lodge. There was blood on my feet, but I hadn't noticed. The only thing I could feel was the pain in my children's cries.

The worst had happened.

One

I looked down nervously at the white envelope on the hall floor. Could it be the dreaded exam results? I hesitated, but then slowly bent down and picked up the envelope, opening it like it contained a bomb. Sliding out the piece of paper inside, until I saw the words 'PASS'. My heart leapt with a mixture of relief and joy. I was now the proud owner of a post grad marketing diploma. I jumped up in the air, arms stretched overhead.

'Yes!' I shrieked.

I poured myself a glass of chilled white wine and carried it into my bedroom. Putting my Justin Timberlake CD on play and sitting down in front of the mirror, I carefully applied eyeliner, mascara, bronzer and fuchsia pink lipstick before straightening my long, dark hair. I pulled on a pair of tight black jeans, a black and green strappy top and stepped into a pair of black shiny stilettos. Spraying a mist of Angel perfume on my wrists and neck, delicious vanilla and patchouli filled the air, reminding me of marshmallows. A car beeping outside told me my lift had arrived. Grabbing my handbag, mobile phone and my small leather jacket, I headed outside into a dark, rainy Manchester evening.

It was Friday night, and I was meeting up with a group of mates. I was looking forward to a few drinks. Smiling, I walked across the square and headed down a little side street to the pub. The music gradually became louder as I climbed the stairs down to the small, smoke filled basement bar. Immediately, I spotted my friends who were huddled round a couple of tables in a dark corner.

A few minutes later, Damian arrived. *Was he the one that Alison fancied?*

'My round – what's everyone drinking?' he asked.

There was a chorus of replies, and moments later he had returned with the drinks.

'Mandy, a gin and tonic sounded like a good idea'

He handed me my drink, and also placed his gin and tonic down. He pulled the chair out at the side of me.

'Mind if I sit here next to you?' he asked, smiling.

'Of course. Sit down,' I replied.

Damian was friendly and easy to talk to, and we seemed to have a lot in common. We were both vegetarian. He talked about a new restaurant that had just opened.

'We should go?' he suggested.

I smiled. 'Yes, definitely.' *Wasn't he gay, though?*

We told each other about our lives, interests, and what we did for work. He reminded me of an excited little boy.

'Believe it or not, I used to be a fox hunt saboteur,' he confessed, blushing slightly.

I giggled. It was quite hard to believe. He looked too strait-laced, but the thought pulled at my heart strings. I got up from my chair to head for the toilets.

'I love that man!' I declared to my friends, walking past them.

Damian smiled coyly and looked at his feet.

As I was washing my hands, Alison suddenly appeared at the side of me.

'Is there someone you like here?' she asked, her words slightly slurred, looking up at me with her big eyes.

I realised she was trying to find out if I was attracted to Damian.

'No, of course not!' I answered, a bit too quickly. I thought he was quite fit, but he was a bit nervy and erratic and not really my type. In any event, Alison fancied him so he was off limits.

As the evening progressed, a larger group of friends joined us, and Damian suggested we head over to a night club. Once at the club, we danced to Northern Soul music and drank and laughed and chatted. I noticed Damian was dancing close by, and I got the impression that he was attracted to me. A couple of drinks later, Sally and Liz announced they were leaving.

'Come back to mine,' Sally suggested, drunkenly. 'I have lots of wine. Tell everyone to come.' With that, they promptly left. A few more of the group had also hit the road, and all that remained was Alison and me, Damian, and a couple of Damian's friends.

'Come to Sally's house, she's having a few people over!' I yelled at Alison, over the music.

'No, I'm not going to bother, I'm tired, I'm just going to go home now,' Alison yelled back, grabbing her coat.

My eyes met Damian's.

'Do you want to come back to Sally's? Your friends are invited too.' I shouted to be heard over Frank Wilson's, "Do I Love You?", which was blasting out of the speakers.

'Yeah sure, count us in.' He smiled.

***

Me, Damian, and his friends piled into a taxi. I phoned

Sally. 'We're on our way,' I told her.

'I'm not going to bother now, Mandy,' she said. 'Sorry, very drunk.'

Okay, I had to come up with another plan.

'Come to mine?' I suggested to the small group. 'I've got wine and music.'

I began humming, "Do I Love You". *It was going be stuck in my head all night!*

'Sounds all right, mate,' Johnny, Damian's loudest friend, enthused.

Everyone was in agreement, but just a couple of minutes later, Johnny started an argument with the taxi driver. It seemed to come from nowhere. The taxi driver was having none of it, and promptly stopped the car.

"Get out now!" he ordered Johnny. His two mates quickly followed suit, until only Damian and I were left in the taxi.

'Guess it's just us two then.' Damian smiled at me, shyly.

'Guess so,' I replied, allowing my head to fall on his shoulder.

Once in my flat, I poured us both a glass of wine. Damian was sat to one side of my large sofa, in the centre of my living room.

'Nice flat,' he commented, looking around at the ultra -modern glass furnishings and boldly coloured sofa with matching curtains.

'I can't take the credit for that. I just rent a room.'

I handed him a glass, put some music on and walked over, kicking off my shoes and settled in beside him. The conversation flowed, and I found myself laying my feet casually across his lap. Damian leaned over to me, his mouth searching for mine, and we began kissing passionately.

4

The following morning, I awoke with a dull head and a dry mouth. I glanced over at the man asleep in bed next to me. *What was I thinking? Jumping into bed with a total stranger... Does he do this every weekend?* I could feel my cheeks getting hot. Damian stirred, I glanced over towards him.

'Morning!' I tried to sound bright.

'Well good morning to you too.' He smiled, pulling me towards him, and showered me with affection. Soon, we were cuddling and laughing. The fears that I had woken up to were fading away.

It was late morning before Damian left. He lingered at the door, wrapping my hair around his index finger, his eyes refusing to leave my face. It was flattering, but a bit disconcerting. Still, when he asked for my number, I didn't hesitate. Closing the door, I leaned up against it, my mind a whirlpool of emotions. I was excited to be at the start of something, frightened because I'd never met anyone like him, and a little dizzy, though that could have been the hangover. I filled a glass with water and swallowed it in a couple of mouthfuls. Another emotion crept in—guilt. I had just spent the night with a man that Alison had been attracted to for about a year.

Damian began texting me straight away. I received the first one less than an hour after he left. *He must be keen. Was he a bit too keen? And intense? But exciting too! It made me feel wanted.*

We arranged our next date for the following Friday evening. Damian asked if I wanted to go for dinner.

'I'll meet you in The Liar's Club,' he suggested. 'It's one of my favourite bars in town.'

'Okay, sounds good to me.' I couldn't wait!

***

Friday night finally arrived. Leaving my house in a new pair of jeans and my blue silk blouse, my hair freshly styled, I conceded I was very excited about my first date with Damian. I arrived at the bar a couple of minutes late. As I walked through the door, I noticed him immediately. He was wearing a black duffle coat and reading a copy of *The Guardian*. He looked up when I opened the door and smiled. My heart skipped a beat. He threw the newspaper down and walked towards me, giving me the biggest hug. He pulled me tight into him. It felt so nice and safe and warm.

'Lovely to see you! You look beautiful.' He looked deep into my eyes as he spoke.

'It's good to see you too.' I blushed.

'What are you having?' he asked. 'I got some wine, chardonnay, like in your house.'

I wasn't planning to drink, but he'd been kind enough to think of me.

'Chardonnay's great.' I smiled as he handed me a glass.

A few glasses later, I was hungry and keen to get away from the crowded bar.

'I thought we could try out that new veggie restaurant that's just opened,' Damian suggested, as if reading my mind. 'But let's have one more drink before we go. Shall I surprise you?'

What the heck? We could eat after one more; we'd be even hungrier.

Damian had switched from wine to cocktails. 'You look like a 'Sex on the Beach' sort of girl.' He grinned, placing a large cocktail in front of me.

One cocktail led to two and the night slowly turned into a big blur, with the odd flash of us snogging and laughing and chatting away in different bars. I'm pretty sure we didn't eat anything. Either way, when I woke up snuggled next to him the following morning it felt so right, and I was beginning to feel like I might have finally met a serious match.

***

Damian and I very quickly became an item. It was spring 2003. I was twenty-six, and he was twenty-nine. He would constantly send me charming texts telling me how gorgeous and amazing I was. Every time I heard my phone ping, I would be swarmed with more messages from him. *I can't wait to see you Mandy…I can't stop thinking about you, beautiful woman… One more day before we see each other… I can't sleep thinking about you so much.*

***

One night we were standing in my kitchen. He had just arrived to pick me up and take out for tapas at a local Spanish restaurant. He had brought a package and handed it to me.

'I made you this. You said you liked bread.'

I opened the package and looked at the white loaf. Freshly baked bread that he had made himself. It was still warm, and the delicious smell filled the room. It was such a sweet and romantic gesture. I placed the loaf on the work top, turned around and wrapped my arms around him. After a few seconds, he pulled back and placed his hands on the sides of my arms. He looked at me intently.

'Will you be my girlfriend?' he asked in a hushed voice.

I felt my knees go weak. 'Yes!' I exclaimed.

It felt like something out of a movie. No one had ever asked me to be their girlfriend, officially before. I'd had boyfriends, but they'd never officially sought permission. I felt so safe and secure with Damian, so certain that we were both committed. He made me feel like a princess, and we had the best time together. Every week he would take me out for dinner, at least a couple of times, and pretty soon we had eaten at every single restaurant in Manchester. We laughed at the same things, and I liked how he could laugh at himself too. Sometimes he reminded me of a little boy who wasn't quite sure of himself. He could be clumsy and drop things. Once, when we were out in a bar, he wandered into the women's toilets by accident. He was always doing things like that. We would joke about it, afterwards, and I would be in stitches. Damian, despite often being the butt of the jokes, laughed hardest of all. I loved that he had a good sense of humour and didn't take himself too seriously.

'It feels so new with you,' Damian would tell me, constantly.

***

Damian and I had been dating for a couple of weeks when he invited me to a lodge in the Lake District, for a romantic weekend away. It was owned by his family and used exclusively by them and their close friends. It seemed significant that he wanted to take me there so soon.

The lodge was cosy and quaint. It was the size of a small bungalow, with an open plan kitchen/lounge/diner, decorated in typically eighties décor. I guessed that it hadn't been refurbished since then. The carpets were faded, and the sofas well worn. There was a sheepskin rug in front of the fire. It had three small bedrooms and a bathroom with a large, round bath. A framed photograph of teenager Damian and his family hung above the fireplace. I giggled at his long black hair. His father was positioned on a chair, his mother stood to the side of him. Damian and his sister sat on the floor, underneath their father, along with their pet German Shepherd. It was very clear who the head of the family was.

On the second day, the weather was glorious, so we went for a walk. At the edge of the lake we paused for a few minutes, stood together holding hands and looking in amazement at the breath-taking views of the water, with the backdrop of green hills and bright blue sky. The lake was completely still, like glass. There was barely a ripple. The hills covered in green. The smell of freshly cut grass reminded me of my childhood. I felt the warm sun on my face. There was not another soul in sight. At that point in time, it felt like we were the only people on the planet.

'We should take a snapshot of this moment in our minds and keep it safe in our memories,' Damian whispered, squeezing my hand, as we stared out in amazement at the views.

He had totally swept me off my feet.

***

I'd always been very close to my family, especially Mum and Naomi, my younger sister, so I couldn't wait for Damian to meet them. I felt sure they'd be as beguiled by him as I was, and I was right. Mum and him immediately hit it off, even sharing a similar taste in music. They lost me when they started talking about their love of soul. I rolled my eyes in embarrassment. Soul music certainly wasn't my cup of tea. My dad seemed to take to him, in his own way, as did Grandad. Damian had charmed everyone. He had made an immediate impression and found a way to share common ground with each of them.

'I really like him,' my sister Naomi confided in me, after he left.

I grinned from ear to ear. My family's approval, and especially Naomi's, meant the world to me.

***

It was clear from early on in our relationship that Damian was something of a party animal, with an appetite for booze and drugs.

'I'm going to a rave in London next weekend,' he announced one morning, when we were in bed. 'I don't think you'd like it, babe. Everyone will be on drugs, so, I'm going to go on my own, yeah?'

He posed it like a both a question and answer.

'No, I probably wouldn't,' I replied. I couldn't help thinking it would have been nice to be asked.

He chuckled and nudged me with his elbow. 'I think I'm much more of a partier than you are, bless your cotton socks.'

I laughed along, even though I didn't get the joke.

***

Although Damian was an extrovert and very confident in many ways, he had an insecure side and would sometimes send me to the bar to get the drinks when we were out. Getting all flustered, he would thrust a pile of notes into my hand.

'I can't speak properly,' he'd croak, mouth downturned in the corners, like a nervous little boy.

Though this impression of being vulnerable and childlike was at odds with his more confident side, I found it quite endearing. He had a stammer that would sometimes make an appearance when he was nervous. It always seemed to move me. Here was a man who unafraid to acknowledge his insecurities. That was a positive quality, surely?

***

'I can't wait for you to meet my family; shall we go next weekend?' Damian asked, when we'd been together for a couple of months.

'This weekend's good for me,' I replied casually, careful that my voice didn't betray my excitement. He was finally introducing me to his folks. We were getting serious.

'So, what are they like then?" I asked, tentatively. Despite being welcomed into my home early on, Damian had always been more resistant about his background. I didn't push it, but I was curious. 'Who do you take after?'

'Dad, definitely,' Damian replied. 'Dad's very liberal. He's my main role model. Mum and Sarah are more conservative.'

'Who's Sarah again?'

'My sister,' Damian replied.

I felt a twinge of fear as I realised how little I knew about him. That would all change now that I was meeting the parents.

'Mum's a natural healer, She's a Mother Theresa. She always has 'waifs and strays' back at the house.' Damian continued. He was trying to sound light, but I could sense an edge to his voice.

***

The following Saturday I met Damian's family for the first time. Damian seemed unusually quiet that morning. 'What's up?' I asked.

'Nothing at all,' he replied.

'You haven't said a word all morning. Are you nervous?'

'No.' He laughed. 'Far from it.'

'Good. Parents usually like me.'

Damian parked the car outside his sister's house. Taking a deep breath, I climbed out of the car. I stood slightly behind Damian as he rang the doorbell. Sarah, who was heavily pregnant with her second baby, answered the door.

'Hi bro!' She hugged Damian. 'Come on in, you two.'

She smiled then quickly began looking me up and down; she seemed to be giving me a once over. *Was I dressed appropriately?*

'You must be Mandy.'

'Yes, and you must be Sarah, lovely to meet you.' I walked, nervously, through into the living room.

A few enquiring faces looked up at me. A small, slightly rounded looking woman with short jet-black hair and tanned skin walked over to me, arms outstretched and gave me a hug. The hug felt slightly forced.

'It's lovely to finally meet you, Mandy, I'm Jean. We've heard a lot about you.' Her greeting was warmer than Sarah's.

'Me too,' I lied.

A little boy was tapping on a toy keyboard, at the back of the settee.

'I'm Timothy,' he introduced himself. He was adorable, with a shock of dark brown hair, smiley eyes and a cheeky grin.

'He's gorgeous,' I said, smiling over at Sarah, who sat yawning on a chair.

'I'll let you decide who's gorgeous after you've spent a day looking after him.' Sarah chuckled.

'Damian looks after Timothy a lot, don't you, bro?'

I gave him a warm look. Funny, thoughtful, good with kids, he kept growing in my esteem.

Damian's dad, Bill, was nothing like I thought he'd be. He was huge, for a start, and quite gruff. He was sitting in a single recliner chair, with a cup propped on his enormous belly, as if it was a shelf.

'Does she bring you breakfast in bed, son?' he croaked up in a loud, husky voice.

'Every morning,' Damian laughed.

The sexist nature of Bill's question didn't go unnoticed and neither did Damian's glib reply.

'Is he behaving himself, Mandy?' He looked over at me.

I faked a smile. 'Yes, I think so.'

I wasn't sure what to make of his questions. I glanced over at Damian; his expression gave nothing away.

'Fine looking lad, isn't he, Mandy?' Bill continued,

glancing over at Damian. 'Looks like his dad, don't you think?'

He patted the same belly previously used as a table to emphasise his point. I forced another laugh. It wasn't my kind of humour, but I wanted to be polite to the father of my boyfriend.

***

Just like Damian kept me at arm's length from his family, he did the same with his work life. I knew he worked with his dad. I knew his dad was in business; I knew he had an office. I knew his dad was nearing retirement. I knew he always had money. I knew their work involved lots of travel, the bulk of which fell on the younger, fitter Damian.

'Why do you have to go to Holland and Belgium all the time?' I asked him, before yet another last-minute trip.

'To show the customers around the factories,' he replied.

He never really explained why the customers were so keen to see the factories where their products were sourced. Like most conversations involving work, he quickly changed the subject. 'Pete and Kate are up for the weekend. Shall I book us a foursome for dinner?'

I nodded. I didn't like pressing him on stuff.

Damian adored his friends, and this feeling seemed reciprocated. He would lavish them with attention and affection. He was always the one buying rounds, remembering birthdays and important events, making toasts, lavishing praise, with just the right touch of self-deprecating humour. Initially, it was another thing to like about him, his financial and emotional generosity, but after a few months, it got tiring. Damian's compulsion to be the social glue that held his otherwise diverse set of friends together seemed to outweigh his commitment to me. In spite of his huge social appetite, Damian wasn't so keen on me doing my own thing.

'I'll come over to yours after the gym, babe.' I was about to go to my usual Tuesday night boxercise class. There was a pause on the other end of the phone.

'You're going to the gym, again? You've already been twice this week,' he eventually replied.

'What? I don't understand, Damian. Why does that bother you?'

'It bothers me because you should be coming out more, socially, with me,' was his stern reply.

'But I do go out with you lots,' I said.

'Look, if you carry on like this, then I will have no option but to end our relationship. I'll leave it with you.'

The phone went dead.

My eyes welled up. I felt confused, hurt and misunderstood. *Why was he so bothered about me going to the gym?*

***

We had been together for about eight months when Damian asked me to move in with him.

'Yes,' I said instantly.

Sure, we had our problems, but I'd never had a boyfriend as serious as Damian, and I was excited about the prospect of us setting up home together. He had bought a new house on the other side of Manchester and was in the process of renovating it. It was going to take a lot of work to modernise. The previous owner, an old lady, had passed away. Walls were being taken down, a new kitchen and bathroom were being fitted, new floors, new doors, the lot!

Things would improve then once we had moved in together and started sharing decisions. We could get a couple of rescue cats and grow some organic veg in the garden. I imagined us, in matching overalls, planting rows of asparagus, and using the more expensive but humane netting to keep out the rabbits.

'We can throw dinner parties for our friends,' I suggested, as we surveyed our new home, together, for the first time.

'Yes, babe, we can get someone over every week. Impress them with our culinary skills.' He pulled me close to him, kissing my neck. 'Let's stay here for a couple of years, and then get somewhere bigger, get married and have lots of children.'

'One step at a time,' I replied, laughing, but secretly I was pleased that Damian was thinking ahead. We both appeared to be on the same page and wanting the same things.

***

Within a few months of moving in, the cracks in our relationship began to surface, just as surely as the cracks on the wall turned smooth. We had little in common, and co-habitation emphasised our differences. Damian never asked me anything about myself, or my childhood, or my opinions, or my thoughts. In fact, if he wasn't asking me where I wanted to go, or what colour I wanted a wall, we were barely talking. It was always me starting the harder conversations about feelings and intimacy. He would shut these down with jokes or a pass. It was always me moving us from fickle topics (like his prolific drug taking tall tales) to serious issues like the state of the world and animal's rights. When we first met, he couldn't get enough of saving whales and protecting endangered species. He was always forwarding me petitions and demo details. Now the conversation provoked a patronising sneer.

'That's what I love you,' he'd proffer, when I suggested we join Naomi and her friends on a march. 'You find space to care about everything.'

It should have been a compliment, but there was pitying tone to his delivery. I bored him. My whole life bored him. Least that's how it appeared. My family, whom he was once so keen to court, bored him. When we were at my mum's or my sister's or even Dad's, he would be strangely quiet constantly making excuses to leave—we had to get back for the cats, we had to get back for a delivery, we had an early start the next day.

I loved my family, and I was hurt that Damian didn't. I also felt a bit cheated. We'd moved in together on the understanding that I came from close knit roots. It was as if he was trying to loosen the very ties he'd once envied.

'I know what you're going to say.' He slunk into the driver's seat, after another afternoon visit cut short by his desperate need to check in with the plumber. 'I find your family hard work, Mandy, and a bit provincial. It's not their fault; I'm used to more worldly people.'

I hesitated, desperate to retaliate, unable to form words. 'Where are we on the carpeting for the spare bedroom?' I eventually spoke. 'I know you'd prefer grey, but I think aqua is warmer.'

***

The following Friday night I had given the gym a miss so I could join Damian and his friends for an evening out watching live music.

'So glad you're coming, babe,' Damian said in the taxi en route. 'It'll be fun.'

He looked me up and down.

'You've done me proud, babe, you look sexy in that skirt.'

I smiled coyly.

As we walked into the smoky, warehouse style venue, Damian spotted some of his friends. 'Hi, everyone, this is Mandy,' he announced.

Engaging in small talk with one of the group, I noticed Damian walking away and chatting with a man. They looked friendly. They were heading towards the bar.

'I'm going to the bar to get a drink, anyone want one?' I asked his three friends.

Everyone was okay. I walked over to the bar, close to where Damian and the man stood.

'Hi, just a gin and tonic please,' I asked the barman. Damian appeared at my side.

'Mandy, I am just going to catch up with Pete. I'll come and find you in ten mins, okay?' Damian said.

'Okay.' I hesitated, before heading back to Damian's friends. We chatted for another twenty minutes before Paul headed to the bar.

'Fancy another drink?' he offered.

'Yes, please. I'll have a G&T.'

'No, thanks,' replied Jim. 'I have to be up early tomorrow. Good meeting you, Mandy.' That was the most words he'd spoken all evening.

Another half an hour passed. There was only so much chit-chat me and Paul could manage.

'I'm going to try and find Damian now.' I hastily moved towards the bar.

Wandering around the crowded room, I couldn't see Damian anywhere. I shuffled my way through the couples and groups of people and headed for the bar.

'Double G&T please,' I slurred. I pulled a stool up to the bar and spent the rest of the night sitting on my own.

'You left me all night!' I finally shouted when we got home.

'That's unfair, Mandy. I introduced you to my friends as soon as we got there. It's up to you to make the effort with people,' he responded, walking upstairs.

I couldn't sleep a wink that night. *Why was he like this*

with me? Where had he been all night? Why hadn't he come to look for me, once? Who the heck was Pete? I'd never heard of him before. Actually, I'd never heard of any of tonight's friends before. Who were any of them? And the question my drunken mind couldn't escape, who the heck was Damian?

***

Whilst distancing me from my family, Damian contrived events, so we spend more time with his.

Near the end of the summer, we were invited, with his family, to the retirement 'do' of an ex colleague, working in the same industry. It was held at a grand hotel in Harrogate. Bill had been asked to give a speech.

Everyone clapped their hands as Bill made his way to the front of the room. About twelve large round tables filled the space, with ten guests sat around each one. The room had high, decorative ceilings with crystal chandeliers hanging from them. Through the enormous windows where impressive views of the manicured gardens.

Damian leaned over to me and whispered in my ear. 'Babe, remember to tell Dad how good his speech was. He loves the praise; it'll mean a lot to him.'

He squeezed my hand and nodded. I forced a smile. 'Okay,' I replied.

The clapping stopped and Bill, holding a piece of paper with his notes on, began his speech. 'Well, I have to say, it's an honour to be invited to speak at the retirement do for my oldest friend. To be fair, Brian was an old codger twenty years ago, when he should have retired…'

The audience laughed. His speech was peppered with humorous insults as well as compliments. When he finished, Damian and his mum sprang to their feet to give him a standing ovation. Damian looked down at me, glaring. I stood up too.

'So, how did I do?' Bill addressed the table as he sat down.

'Fantastic, Dad, couldn't fault it,' Damian eagerly replied.

'You did amazing, Bill, as always,' said his mum.

Bill looked straight at me.

'That was very good, Bill, well done,' I said, trying to feign enthusiasm.

We had to sit through a few more speeches until the food was served. The evening continued with a string quartet and more wine, until we were ready to leave. As we were saying our goodbyes, Bill announced to everyone in his loud, croaky voice. 'I had better have a mint, as I'll be kissing my lovely daughter when I get home.'

Damian laughed. Nobody else did.

***

On top of his growing disdain for my family, and new-found appreciation for his own, I also had to contend with Damian's partying. He was very much still part of a lifestyle most folk leave behind in their twenties. He would regularly take cocaine and ecstasy.

It was a Friday night, just after Halloween, we were at a house party of a friend of Damian's. The basement had been converted into a nightclub style set up, dark and dingy. A DJ had been hired, and loud drum and base was pumping through the house. It was well into the evening, and a man who had been dancing at my side, for over an hour, moved closer, and started chatting me up. Damian was close by. The man became more and more flirtatious, and I became more uncomfortable, not with the bloke's flirting, but with Damian's clear disinterest. Don't get me wrong, I didn't want him causing a scene, or creating trouble, but I also didn't want him so oblivious as not to notice.

Breaking free from the attentive stranger, I took a seat in the corner and eyed up Damian. He hadn't noticed I'd left. He hadn't noticed another man wanting me. I cast my mind back to a festival he'd taken me to, at the start of summer. We'd all had a few beers, and I was talking to Damian's friend, Carl. Damian was to our right, leaning on a car, soaking up the sun.

A bee buzzed round my hair, and I started to scream. Carl waved his hand slowly in the bee's direction, and it flew away. We both burst out laughing. Pointing to Damian, lying on the car bonnet, he told me, 'You are so wasted on that guy. He wouldn't care if I kissed you, right here, right now. Watch this, you'll see what I mean.'

Carl leaned in to kiss me on the lips. I backed away, all the while my eyes fixated on Damian's reaction. There was none. Carl was right! Damian didn't move a muscle. One of his friends had hit on me, right in front of him, and Damian had neither noticed nor cared.

**

The longer we were together the more I wasn't sure why we were. I began to doubt myself and wonder if I'd ever be "enough" for him. Maybe I was too dull? Too mature? He seemed to find me boring. We never talked unless I instigated it, and even then, he never appeared interested in my ideas or in my opinions. For me, being in a couple meant sharing your thoughts and dreams. I struggled to hold Damian's attention for long enough to express mine, let alone hear his. This wasn't what I signed up for. I wondered why he stayed with me. It didn't add up. He couldn't be happy with the way things were, surely? The Damian that I'd first met no longer existed. I would see how he was with other people, and it reminded me of how he used to treat me. When I tried to talk to him about our incompatibility, he would laugh it off and say that I was being silly. And maybe I was? Maybe I was expecting too much from him?

***

'We don't talk anymore,' I said, out of the blue to him, one Sunday morning as we were eating a fully English veggie breakfast at our local cafe.

Damian laughed! 'It's so fu-nny how we don't talk anymore!' He started singing the Cliff Richard song. Then he wrapped his arm clumsily around me and pulled me close. 'You're too serious, Mandy, you need to lighten up.'

He laughed some more.

I laughed as well because I didn't know what else to do.

***

The following spring, we were at a friend's wedding reception sitting around a table full of other couples who were engaging in conversation with one another. I looked at Damian, who was looking everywhere, apart from at me.

'I am here, you know,' I said, hoping I didn't sound as pathetic as I felt.

'Ha, I know, babe! I'm just people watching. I do love you, you know?'

Only I didn't know, and every time I sought reassurance, I came away less sure.

***

It was October 2005 and we set off on a two-week trip travelling around India with Damian's Mum, Jean and two of her sisters. Jean had emigrated to England when she was eight years old. She and her sisters wanted to revisit the land of their birth. I felt humbled to be asked on such a personal voyage. Damian had planned the trip, including stays in Delhi, Mumbai, Agra, Nagpur and Shimla.

Apart from one plane journey, we travelled across the country by train. It was an eye-opening experience. In Delhi, I was struck by the poverty and the chaos on the roads. I gasped when I saw a woman sat on the back of a motorbike holding a tiny baby and tried not to weep every time another toddler pulled at my clothes and begged.

'It's an explosion of the senses isn't it, Mandy? All the colours, and the smells,' Jean confided in me. She didn't seem to notice the depravity or the desperation in people's faces, or if she did, it didn't seem to affect her.

Our Indian experience couldn't have been more different than that of the locals. We stayed in four- and five-star hotels, even some suites. We got to ride up the Himalayas on a 'toy' train. It was an adventure. I was honoured to be a part of Jean and her sister's reminiscing. We took in some of the more touristy sights, including the Taj Mahal. It was the most magnificent building I had ever seen. I stared in awe. A group of young Indian girls swarmed around me, asking if they could take a photo. I happily agreed.

After a few photos, Damian took my hand and sat me down around the corner on a bench. He looked straight at me. 'Will you marry me?' he asked in almost a whisper.

I was struggling to get my head round his question. *Marriage? Us? Really?* A tiny voice, at the back of my mind, was screaming, *"No!"*

'Yes,' I heard myself say, throwing my arms around him. It was such a grand gesture, and such a romantic setting, and whatever the tiny voice in my head was saying didn't really matter.

Two

We were only a week back from our Indian excursion when Damian brought me a coffee in bed.

'Thank you honey.' I sat up and sipped the hot coffee.

'I don't want one of those long engagements,' Damian said, gently pushing back a stray hair from my face. 'I want you to be my wife right now, babe.' *How romantic.*

'What's got into you?' I asked, smiling.

The following Saturday afternoon we were sitting at the dining table which was covered with bridal magazines.

'Do you like this dress, love?' I glanced at Damian.

'I think you'd look good in any old thing.' He smiled, leaning over to stroke my cheek. 'I love planning our wedding together, babe. We make a fine team, don't we?'

At last, we seemed to have stumbled across a project we could really connect on. It was as if Damian was born to plan a wedding. After work, every evening, our time was spent writing lists, visiting potential venues and pulling together what would be a truly magical day. We were completely caught up in the excitement of it all; trying on dresses and suits, choosing flowers, tasting food for the menus, hen and stag dos, deciding who to invite, and which exotic location to spend our honeymoon in. So swift was our organising, that in no time at all, we were counting down the days.

The morning arrived, and it was a perfect mid Summers day. I awoke to the sun peeping in through the cracks of the blinds. Rubbing my eyes, I climbed out of bed and looked out of the window. The sky was completely blue, without a cloud in sight. Moments later, I heard Naomi's voice from downstairs.

'Coffee's ready!'

The patio doors to the garden were wide open. Naomi was sitting at the outside table.

'You nervous?' She grinned at me.

'More excited,' I replied, half truthfully.

'Me too.' She smiled, sipping her coffee.

We sat with the hot sun on our faces for a few minutes.

'Here, make sure you have something to eat.' Naomi said, passing me a plate of hot buttered toast, which I gobbled down.

'I'd better go and get showered and ready then!' I jumped up in excitement and pulled Naomi to her feet.

'Okay, bride to be!' She laughed.

Taking the stair two at a time, I got first dibs on the bathroom. The next couple of hours were like a military operation, as we showered, had our hair and make-up done, and fielded a string of last-minute texts about the arrangements.

About one o'clock people started to slowly arrive. Mum was the first.

'Mum, you look beautiful' I said.

'You too' Mum chuckled, eying my cut off t-shirt and shorts.

'Very funny. Come and help me on with my dress.'

The dress was the last thing to do. It was a fairy tale ball gown with billowing skirts and a fitted corset. Having helped tie the corset up, Mum stepped back to admire me.

'Mandy, you look like a princess,' she said, wiping a tear from her eye.

'Where's the bride to be?' I heard a voice yell from downstairs.

'Hi Dad!' Naomi and I called out in unison.

He was waiting with my other bridesmaid, Isabel.

As I walked carefully down the stairs, he gave me a reassuring thumbs up.

The flowers had also arrived, stunning bouquets of delicately scented roses, the centre of each dotted with a glistening diamante. Picking them up and handing them out to Mum and the girls, I was walking on air. This was the wedding I'd always dreamed of.

***

After the first car had arrived to collect Mum and the bridesmaids, it was just Dad and I left. We giggled, as we sipped a little brandy to steady our nerves.

'How are you feeling?' he asked.

'A bit anxious but so excited. I can't believe I'm getting married!'

My dad gave me a wry smile and I could see the sadness at the back of his eyes.

Within fifteen minutes our car had arrived. The drive over was surreal. I couldn't quite believe it. *Was I really getting married today?*

My bridesmaids were standing outside the impressive entrance of the Town Hall. Taking a deep breath, I gathered up my skirts and climbed out of the car.

Naomi wiped a tear from her eyes. 'Mandy, you look beautiful.'

The registrar greeted us on the way in.

'Your groom awaits,' a woman, with a booming voice, announced.

I made my way up the stone staircase, my bridesmaids in tow and Dad at my side, smiling as I noticed the lit tea lights and rose petals that had been arranged on the windowsills. Approaching the doorway at the end of the corridor, we heard the soft sound of violins. As we entered the room, the guests started to turn around. My heart raced as the band played, "Cannon in D". My eyes travelled to the other side of the room where Damian stood. He gave me a reassuring nod. Behind him, in the front row, his father stood. His face was rigid as if he was at a funeral not a wedding.

Before I knew it, I was standing next to my husband to be. The registrar started talking. I couldn't take in what she was saying. *I can't believe I'm getting married.* The best man passed Damian the ring. We both said something, then I heard the words, 'You may now kiss your bride,' and Damian pulled me towards him and gave me a full-on snog.

***

A couple of days later we jetted off on honeymoon to beautiful Mauritius. It was pure luxury. An all-inclusive resort on the coast with white sands, aqua seas and state of the art swimming pools. On our first morning, we drank fresh coffee and ate a breakfast of delicious fresh fruits and pancakes before heading down for a swim. As we walked down the path and onto the pool area, Damian turned around.

'There aren't any kids. It must be one of those resorts that don't allow children.'

'Good, it'll be nice and peaceful,' I said.

'I can't wait to have my own children.' He smiled.

We settled on a couple of sun loungers, and a waiter immediately appeared out of nowhere asking if we would like a drink. A couple of cocktails later, we lay outstretched, listening to the sound of the gentle waves. We spent our days sunbathing, drinking cocktails and reading books.

'This is heaven.' Damian stroked my hand. 'I love spending time with you.'

'Me too, babe,' I replied.

After a day of lounging around we would get dressed for the evening. First, we would have dinner, followed by cocktails, followed by table football in the games room.

'I'm not leaving until I've won!' Damian declared.

I laughed. 'No chance, we'll be here all night in that case!'

Damian came over to my side of the table, grabbing my hand and pulling me away out of the room. 'Come on, wifey, we've got a baby to go and make!'

I giggled. 'But I thought you couldn't leave until you'd beaten me.'

***

Once our relaxing honeymoon came to an end, we returned home to start our lives as a married couple. It was a typically dark and dreary November, and visions of our sun-drenched perfect holiday faded fast. Damian's hints and jokes about impregnating me had morphed into a sort of obsession. He paced up and down the kitchen. *Had he always paced like this?*

'Why aren't you pregnant yet?' he asked for the fiftieth time.

It was all he seemed to think about.

'Chill out it's only been a few months, Damian. Give it a chance.'

'Well, I don't want to take any chances, Mandy. We need to go to the doctors and get checked out. I need to get my sperm count tested first. That's what they usually do before anything else.' Clearly, he'd done his homework.

'We've been trying for such a short time, babe,' I spoke softly. 'The professionals are going to say the same as I have been, "give it a while longer".'

'Good point!' Damian seized on my analysis. 'We need to tell the doctors that we've been trying for a year, babe, otherwise they might fob us off.'

'I'm starting to think you only married me so that you could have kids.' I poked his ribs as I spoke, and we both laughed.

***

A week later, I was late with my period. An hour later, a pregnancy tester kit confirmed that I was pregnant. Damian could hardly contain himself.

'Yesssss! Get in!!' he shouted. He picked me up and twirled me around. 'Babe, that's amazing, amazing! I'm gonna be a dad.'

I was happy too. I'd worked with kids, I loved them, and I'd always imagined having them. I was also relieved. One thing I'd become certain of was that Damian wasn't going to let up until I sired him an heir.

As soon as the news sunk in, Damian began pushing me to move to a bigger house.

'We need a family home, more room.' He kept telling me.

'Babies are tiny,' I tried to rationalise with him. 'We could actually down-size and the baby won't care.'

My attempts at humour fell on deaf ears. Damian had a plan and was determined to stick to it.

After a couple of months of viewing everything on the market, we had our offer accepted on an impressive four-bedroomed detached house, complete with its own private road. It was a brand-new building that had only been built a couple of years' earlier. I liked it, but I was concerned about the isolation as Damian travelled a lot. There was wasteland and fields directly behind the house. I would be there on my own with the baby.

'What about when you're away, Damian? It's a bit isolated here with no proper neighbours.' I wrung my hands together nervously.

'Don't worry, babe, you'll be safe here. I'll get electric gates. It'll be fine, I promise.'

***

In spite of married life and my pregnancy, Damian continued to party like a single man. He would go out with his friends a lot, as well as travel abroad with his work. I had hoped that after marrying, he would wind things down, but he wasn't showing any signs of giving up his old ways.

It was May 2007, and we decided to have a house-warming for friends and family. The civilised afternoon gathering with a buffet and a few glasses of wine had now turned into a raucous party. Damian's friends were dancing around the lounge, with the music on full blast. There were lines of cocaine on our living room table, and a crowd of people were smoking weed out the back. At about one in the morning, Anne a friend of Damian's from "way back" – *Who wasn't?* – staggered over to me in the kitchen.

'Please can Damian come to the night club?' Anne widened her eyes and fluttered her eyelashes.

I didn't reply, and she wandered off into the hall. A few seconds later, Damian creeped over to me. 'Can I go to the nightclub with them?' Damian giggled, looking back at his small group of friends. Laughter came from the hall, followed by loud shushing and then more laughter. *Was I his wife or his mother?*

'A nightclub?' I could barely lift my face to look at him.

'Yeah, see you later, babe!'

And with a wave of his hand, Damian shuffled off to join his group of wasted mates. I heard the door closing and the sound of hysterical laughter outside. I stood against the ceramic sink, in the brand-new fitted kitchen, heavily pregnant, alone and utterly abandoned.

This was not what I had signed up for.

***

It was on a hot August Sunday when I gave birth to my baby Lewis. The midwife passed me my tiny and precious boy. Holding him, I had never felt love like this before. He seemed to looked up at me. His tiny little fragile arm around mine. I couldn't sleep a wink that night. I kept looking at my perfect little baby boy in his cot at the side of me in the hospital. I felt a happiness and a pure love that I had never felt before.

I was truly blessed with this tiny and perfect baby, but boy, he was exhausting! Getting to grips with the new routine of disturbed sleep and breastfeeding took time, and lots of tears. Lewis was only a week old when Damian first suggested leaving me alone with him.

'I've been offered a once in a lifetime opportunity,' he told me, as our infant son suckled on my breast, 'to meet Ricky Hatton, after a boxing match, in Dublin.' He waited for my reaction. 'Ricky Hatton!' he repeated, having twigged my blank expression.

'Who the heck is Ricky Hatton?' I asked him.

'Ricky Hatton…the boxer.'

It didn't matter how indignant he sounded, I had never heard of the man.

'But, Damian, we've just had a baby. I need help and it's a bit early to leave us.' Panic was creeping in at the thought of me and my tiny baby, without help.

Damian's response was cold. 'I didn't know you were poorly.'

'I'm not poorly.' *Who said anything about being poorly? Lewis was still so small, yet such a big responsibility. Was I being unreasonable?*

Later that evening, he booked a fight to Dublin.

A week later Damian arrived back home from a day at the office. The sun was streaming in through the windows from the back garden, and I was propped up with pillows at the end of a sofa, breastfeeding my hungry baby.

'Mum's going to come and visit for a few days. It will help us having her here, I think.' He sat down on the opposite end of the sofa, unlacing his shoes.

'Okay, yes, that would be good. When is she coming?'

'Tomorrow, babe.' He ruffled my air as he grabbed the television remote control.

Jean arrived the following afternoon.

'I've come to ease the load!' she announced in her shrill voice, as she sailed through the front door.

'I know how difficult it is, especially with your first baby. Here, look, Mandy, I've brought gifts,' she chuckled, pulling out some teddies and baby grows and tea towels from her bag and thrusting them into my arms. I was half grateful for an extra pair of hands and half-wishing she wasn't here.

'Right, son, let's go and buy those wooden clothes hangers,' she said. 'Organising your wardrobe is the first job.'

Damian jumped up, grabbing his coat. 'Told you mum would help, babe.' Kissing me on the cheek, he added, 'Mandy, that's what mothers-in-law are for, to make your life easier.'

The following morning I had just finished feeding Lewis, and after gently placing my baby boy down onto the padded changing table, I twisted the dial on the mobile that hung over him. "Ba-ba-black sheep" started playing when Jean suddenly appeared at my side out of nowhere. She let out a laugh when I jumped.

'Your nerves are all over the place, Mandy' she snorted.

'Good morning Jean.'

Lewis let out a small cry.

'Sorry, sweetheart, let's get this nappy changed.' I stroked his soft downy hair as Jean came closer, peering down at Lewis.

'Makes you wonder how anyone could hurt them, doesn't it, Mandy?'

As a nervous new mum, the very thought of someone harming a tiny helpless new-born baby made me flinch.

'Come on, Mandy, let's go down for a cup of tea.'

I followed Jean out of the room and down the stairs.

'Just wait until you see what I've done with Damian's wardrobe,' she said proudly.

But I didn't care what she'd done with his wardrobe, now all I wanted was her out of my house.

***

New motherhood is the perfect place to hide from marital problems, and I did. I was so engrossed in my baby. I absolutely adored Lewis. His big smile, his baby-scent, his giggle, our cuddles. I whiled away hours staring at him sleeping.

'I've never seen you this happy,' Mum observed. 'You've got a constant smile on your face.'

'It's true, Mum. I'm on cloud nine!' I told her, and I was, except when I thought about Damian, so keen to be father and yet so reluctant.

Mum and Naomi relished in their new roles as Grandma and Aunty. They loved Lewis so much. His little face would light up whenever he saw either of them.

***

As Lewis grew older, Damian and I grew apart though I

was the only one who seemed aware of this. I tried to explain my feelings to Damian, but he'd just dismiss me, with a hug or a ruffle of my hair. Coming in from work one evening, he pulled me close.

'I'm so glad I met you.'

'Me too.'

His words would give me hope for a small time, like hanging on a thread. I would cling to each syllable. *He wouldn't say these things, if he didn't mean them, deep down?*

One night in early summer, Lewis had been asleep for a few hours and I was getting tired. 'I'm going up, honey. Are you coming?'

Damian was sitting back on the sofa, arms outstretched above him. 'I'm going to go and download some music, babe. I'll be up shortly.'

'You never come up at the same time as me,' I said. 'We may as well be sleeping in separate beds.' My eyes filled up with tears.

'Come here, babe.' Damian pulled me gently towards him, smiling. 'I don't care.'

***

'Let's have another baby!' Damian suggested, out of the blue, a few days after Lewis' first birthday.

'No way. Not yet.' I rolled my eyes.

Bringing up baby Lewis was a dream. He was an adorable and happy baby. He slept through the night after only a few weeks. Sometimes, I would even wake up before him in the morning. But I was certainly not ready for another one. There was four years between me and Naomi. I thought that would be a good age gap. It worked well in my family. There was a similar age gap between Damian and his sister, Sarah.

***

Damian's family had recently re-located to Devon.

We would go to stay with them in their thatched cottage in the country at least a couple of times a year. On the one hand, I liked the break from the routine of bringing up baby, but on the other, they had some strange and odd ways about them. On top of that, Damian's dad, Bill, was a typical male chauvinist.

'Dad's very liberal,' Damian would explain, as if I couldn't tell the difference between a liberal man and a sexist pig.

It was plain to see that Bill was the head of the family. He was loud and domineering and reminded me of a large toad. He was also sleazy. Damian had told me a lot about his father.

'My dad had lots of affairs with other women when he was younger.'

'Why didn't your mum leave him?' I asked.

'She did leave him, for about a year. We moved down to Devon when I was about eight and we lived with my aunty.'

'Really? You haven't ever mentioned that before.' I was surprised that Damian had kept something so significant to himself. 'That must have been hard for you?'

'I can't really remember it.' he said.

'So, what made her take your dad back then?' I asked.

'He charmed his way out of it,' Damian replied, half laughing, before quickly changing the subject.

Jean was welcoming and friendly but had a strangeness about her. She would laugh at things that weren't funny and sometimes seemed a bit shrill.

'Mum hasn't been the same since Sarah got married,' Damian told me when I asked about her.

'Why would that be? She likes Stuart.'

'Just hasn't been the same. It all sent her mad.' Damian

shrugged his shoulders.

His reply didn't make any sense to me.

***

Damian wasn't as keen on the reality and responsibility of having a baby as he was on the idea of it. Post the birth of our first child, my life changed beyond recognition. My husband's life, in contrast, continued to be that of a single man. He even joined a band, as a drummer. They met for rehearsal once a week and played the occasional venue.

'We're doing a gig next Saturday, babe. It would be great if you could come.'

'I'd love to!' I agreed immediately. I craved adult company and the chance to be somebody other than a mum.

Naomi agreed to babysit for Lewis for a few hours. I would collect him on the way home. I got dressed up in my tight jeans, a crisp white shirt, and some high heeled strappy sandals. Glancing at myself in the mirror, I was quite pleased. I was looking good, for a new mum, who barely slept or stepped out of my jogging pants.

'You look great, Sis!' Naomi greeted me at the door with a hug. I waited until Lewis had fallen asleep and then drove over to the pub where Damian's band were playing.

'Hi, Mandy!'

Damian's sister, Sarah waved at me. I was relieved to have someone to watch the gig with. We danced, as the band played a few songs. When they paused for a break, I waited for Damian to come over. I spotted him walking towards us.

'Hi, babe, that was amazing,' I told him, but Damian just walked right past me.

Sarah laughed. 'He's a proper charmer, isn't he?'

I nodded, giving her a weak smile.

A few minutes later Damian re-appeared at my side. 'I

have to say babe, I'm disappointed that you're not wearing a skirt,' he whispered.

'What?' I snapped, but he'd already walked away.

'You let me down, babe,' he told me, later that night, when we got back home.

Cradling Lewis in my arms, after I'd fed him, I replayed Damian's words in my mind. I'd disappointed him by not wearing a skirt, that's what he said. *Why would he say that? Why would he even think that?*

***

Somehow, we stumbled on. Me, engrossed with the baby. Damian, being Damian. Lewis's first food, Lewis's first step, Lewis's first word, witnessed by me. That's not uncommon, though, is it? Mums doing the lion share, Dads showing up for the good bits. We weren't perfect, but we were still together.

The following summer, when Lewis was almost two, we went on holiday to the Greek Island, Lindos. On the second week Mum and Naomi joined us.

'Wow, this is so nice!' I exclaimed as we opened the doors to the villa. It was airy and spacious with sea views and its own swimming pool. We walked down to the pool, which was surrounded by a sweet-smelling herb garden. Lewis was absolutely ecstatic at the prospect of all-day swimming. He could hardly contain his excitement.

'Mummy! Look at that! Look at that!' he shouted.

'Look at that!' I repeated, echoing my young son's enthusiasm.

***

'Happy Anniversary.' I handed Damian a card, as he brought the coffee over to the kitchen table in the villa.

'Oh babes, sorry I totally forgot. I was so busy with trying to get things organised at work. I'll make it up to you.

'Don't worry,' I mumbled, conscious that my cheeks were starting to flush.

Who remembers anniversaries after the first?

Mum and Naomi glanced over at me sympathetically.

'Why don't you two go out tonight to celebrate?' Mum suggested.

'Yes, I could look after Lewis,' Naomi said, kissing him on top of his head.

'Fab!' Damian replied.

'Yeah, that would be great,' I told Naomi. 'Thanks.'

After a day on the beach, we got ready for our date, whilst between them, Mum and Naomi made dinner and looked after Lewis. We walked down the steep path, lined with white-washed houses splashed with shocking pink bougainvillea. I reached out to hold Damian's hand.

'Where do you fancy going?' I asked.

'How about that Italian over there?' he suggested.

'A romantic evening out, is it?' the waiter asked us as we sat down.

'It's our third anniversary,' I replied. 'You're quiet,' I said to Damian as I took a slice of pizza from the plate. 'What are you thinking about?'

'Nothing,' he said. 'Pizza's nice, isn't it? Fancy another bottle of merlot?'

'I'm okay, thanks, honey, maybe we could go to another bar for a drink?' *Maybe Damian would liven up then?*

Back in the villa, we said our goodnights to Mum and Naomi and went to bed. I leaned over to kiss my husband.

'I'm tired, babe,' he said, shoving me away. 'Goodnight.'

I rolled over to the edge of my side of the bed feeling unwanted and unloved. We hadn't had sex all holiday. *Why was Damian so distant? Why didn't he want me?*

***

Back home, I was distracted from the problems of my marriage by the problems with Lewis's behaviour. My easy-going baby wasn't negotiating the toddler years so well.

'He's been hitting babies again,' I said to Mum on the phone. 'I'm scared to take him out. I have to have eyes in the back of my head.'

'I'm sure it's just a phase,' Mum tried to reassure me. 'All young kids go through it.'

'Did I?' I asked, hopefully.

'No,' she replied. 'But you were very gentle.'

I didn't tell Mum that we'd started to avoid certain groups and cancel playdates. It was all well and good her saying this was normal, but none of the other toddlers were terrorizing babies.

**

At the beginning of 2010, when Lewis was two and a half, I had quite a few weekends away. This was very unusual for me and I wasn't without misgivings about leaving him, but Damian had been very persuasive.

'You work so hard, babe, and you worry about our boy so much, it will do you good to have some time for yourself,' he told me, when my close friend, Janine, rang to say she wanted to go on a weekend break to Krakow for her hen do.

'I've already been to Bath this year, and to the yoga retreat. I'm not sure I want to leave him again.'

'He'll be with his father,' Damian insisted. 'Or don't you trust me?'

Of course, I trusted him, I just didn't like being away from my baby.

My instincts proved right because when I returned, Lewis seemed unusually subdued. He sat listless on the sofa, barely able to shove a shape through a hole in his favourite toy.

'Did you have a nice time with Daddy, sweetheart?' I asked, stroking his hair.

Damian interjected, 'We've had lots of good fun, Lewis-Daddy time, haven't we, angel?'

Damian fussed over us both, insisting that Lewis needed a nap, and I should have a bath.

I was touched that he was being so attentive, but I craved some alone time with my boy.

'I missed you so much, darling.' I kissed my son's head.

'He was proper wiped out,' I told Damian, after putting Lewis down. 'I haven't seen him crash so easily since he was baby.'

'I had Adam and Jeremy over,' Damian explained. 'We all ran riot in the back garden.'

That made sense of Lewis's exhaustion, but I couldn't help but wonder why two blokes (gay or otherwise) would willingly spend their weekend playing with another bloke's child.

'Jeremy played on your piano,' Damian continued. 'He's very good.'

'Oh, right, is he?' I asked.

***

I was home from Krakow less than a month when I noticed my period was late. We had only just started trying for another baby; I thought these things took a while. They had the first-time round.

Lewis would be turning three soon, which the experts say is a good age for a sibling, but Lewis continued to be not be atypical of his peers. He'd stopped hitting other children, which was good, but he'd developed a terrible stammer.

'What's wrong with Lewis? He seems really down,' Naomi asked, one day when we were out in the garden.

'I don't know,' I replied, and I didn't. No matter how

hard I tried, Lewis never seemed as happy as other kids.

As his days were plagued with a heaviness most three-year-olds didn't seem to carry, it was only a matter of time before these thoughts invaded his nights. Lewis, a one-time fantastic sleeper, started to have nightmares. Every night, without fail, he would scream out and run to my bed before I had time to rise.

'Mummy's here,' I would whisper, wrapping his sweat drenched body round mine. 'You're safe, now.'

He even started to scream about his father putting him to bed. If Damian took him upstairs, within minutes, I would hear Lewis crying, 'No! No! I want Mummy!'

I would rush to my frightened child's side.

'You're not doing him any favours, pandering to his fear of me,' Damian snapped one evening as I held our weeping child.

***

One Sunday morning, towards the end of the Summer. I heard the gates opening at around six am, then the sound of the door closing and footsteps coming up the stairs. I sighed. Damian's social life, already full, seemed to increase with my second pregnancy. *Please don't let him wake Lewis.* Too late! I heard Lewis cry out, and Damian talking to him manically before he took him downstairs. I dragged myself out of bed. He was too wasted to be alone with our son.

'This isn't what I signed up for when we married,' I told him later, when I finally got a wound-up Lewis settled in front of the telly for half an hour.

'Why have *you* got a problem with me having a social life? It's not normal! *You* should go out more yourself! *You* want to take a hard look at yourself," he shouted, before grabbing his wallet and jacket and slamming the door shut as he left.

***

A few days later, Mum was visiting. We had put Lewis to bed and were having a glass of wine.

'Would you like me to have a word with Damian, love?' she asked, her face creased with worry.

'Yes, please, Mum. He might listen to you.'

I was embarrassed asking Mum to intervene on my behalf, but I was also desperate.

Mum went downstairs to the lounge where Damian was sat watching television. I came out onto the landing so I could hear the conversation.

'Damian, I just wondered if we could talk?' I could hear the nervousness in her voice.

'Sure, Dianne. What is it?' Damian replied.

The TV volume was lowered.

'Well, obviously Mandy's pregnant and trying to take care of a toddler, and she needs a lot of help. She doesn't feel supported by you at the moment, and she feels you're always going out. Like the other night, when you got in really late.' Mum spoke slowly. Her voice was gentle and calm. To my shock, I heard Damian shout.

'I don't have to listen to this! Get out of my way!'

Damian was roaring at Mum.

He stormed into the hall, just below where I was stood. I walked downstairs, shaking, deeply regretting allowing Mum try to talk to him.

'Get her out of my house!' he yelled at me.

Tears welled up, and I started to cry. 'No, you get out,' I sobbed. 'Get out now! Mum's been nothing but good to you, and you do this to her.'

He looked at me, eyes glaring. I thought he was going to hit me, and I covered my belly with my arms. 'I'm glad to be getting out of here and away from you,' he spat the words at me.

Mum was shaking. I was crying. Lewis started howling

from upstairs. *What had just happened?*

'He pushed me,' Mum said, her voice unsteady.

'He did *what?*'

I held her close, whispering, "I'm so sorry, Mum," over and over.

I couldn't sleep that night; I couldn't get my head round Damian hurting Mum. I was still awake when I heard the bedroom door creak open and the familiar pattern of footsteps from Lewis. He climbed into my bed and got under the covers. I reached over to his warm body, cuddling him, until he fell asleep in my arms. I inhaled the smell of his hair, and a tear rolled down my cheek.

***

After the assault, Damian stayed with friends for about a month. He would come back to take Lewis out, but we hardly spoke. One evening, he asked if he could come in and talk to me.

'Okay,' I said. 'But I'll need to put Lewis down first.'

We sat on the sofa. Two strangers about to negotiate some kind of truce that would allow us to raise the child we had and the one we were expecting. I'd thought about this moment a lot. When he came back, because everyone said he would, and I had conditions that I wanted in place. I didn't want a husband who still acted like a teenager. I didn't want to walk on eggshells round his mood swings. I certainly didn't want him ever resorting to violence.

'Well, what it is, babe,' Damian began, 'is that I love you, and I can't imagine a life without you. Can I come back?' He reached over for my hand and squeezed it.

'Okay.' I started to sob.

What had happened to my list of demands?

'I'll go and apologise to your mum,' he continued.

'Thank you.' My words were barely a whisper. I was pathetically grateful for the gesture.

'But I could tell that she wanted me to hit her, you know, some women do.' Damian's voice was gentle, his delivery even.

I can't explain why I didn't respond. I was literally lost for words. *Had my husband just accused my Mum of making him hit her?*

If there was ever a time for brushing Damian's behaviour under the carpet, now was the time. I was heavily pregnant and had a lively three-and-a-half-year-old boy to take care of. It was an understatement to say my husband wasn't perfect, but what man is? I allowed him back and I allowed myself believe things would get better.

The first night back, he offered to sleep in the spare room. He said he couldn't sleep properly in our bed together anymore. I didn't counter that I hadn't slept properly since Lewis was born. It was a large house and the spare room was at the opposite end of the corridor next to our boy's room. He said he would get up with Lewis in the mornings.

'It makes things easier for you babe. Give you a bit of a lie in.'

***

It was approaching the end of the year and we were discussing New Year's Eve arrangements.

'Naomi's invited us over for dinner?' I said.

'I'd rather it just be us two,' Damian replied. 'Let's just stay in and have a cosy night together?'

He reached over to squeeze my hand.

On the morning of New Year's Eve, Damian brought me a coffee in bed.

'There you go, babe,' he said, perching on the edge of the bed.

'Shaun's asked me out for a few drinks tonight,' he said. 'I'll only be out for a few hours, then come back, and we

43

can see the new year in together?' Damian stood up and walked out of the room, not even waiting for my reply. That night, Damian said his goodbyes as I was putting Lewis to bed. I went down to watch tv at about nine pm and fell asleep. At midnight, I was awoken to the sound of my phone ringing. It was Mum. We wished each other a happy new year.

'Where's Damian?' she asked, realising that he wasn't with me.

'Oh, he went out for a couple of drinks,' I replied, looking at the empty space on the other side of the sofa. 'I'm sure he'll be back anytime now.'

'Yes, love. Well, I'll see you tomorrow. Good night, God bless.'

Turning the TV off, and heading upstairs, my heart sank as I got into bed, alone on one of the biggest nights of the year. *I had married a total stranger.*

Three

It was a new year, and a new start. We began the year with a new kitchen. The wooden farmhouse style cupboards were painted a Farrow & Ball pale green colour, a new dark floor and white tiles. It looked much better. We would be meeting our new arrival soon. *New babies have a way of making everything alright,* I told myself as I gazed out of the kitchen window, looking at the bare winter trees. *This baby could be just what our family needed to bring it back to life again.*

One cold Saturday afternoon, in February, as I lay on the couch watching television, I felt cramping in my lower abdomen. Lewis was having his afternoon nap.

'I think the baby's coming!' I yelled, with a rush of excitement followed by a wave of fear.

Just over an hour later, my second precious baby boy came into the world. Daniel. I had arranged to have a home birth and that's what I got. The midwife arrived just fifteen minutes before Daniel. She passed me my little bundle. He was darker than Lewis, with big brown eyes, long eyelashes and dark hair. I nestled my new baby and cradled him in my arms. I was besotted. Wrapping him up in a soft blanket, I started to feed him.

'We need to take you to the hospital for some routine checks,' the midwife explained. Baby Daniel and I spent the night in the hospital. I couldn't sleep a wink. I kept looking at my little baby in awe. He was perfect.

Mum, Naomi and Lewis were at home waiting for our arrival.

'Is that the baby, Mummy?' Lewis asked as soon as we walked through the door.

'Yes, sweetheart, this is your baby brother. Sit down on the sofa, and you can hold him if you like?'

Lewis's eyes widened as he climbed onto the sofa.

'Yes, I want to hold him.' Lewis sat patiently at the back of the sofa, looking up at me expectantly. I placed Daniel very gently in his lap. Lewis was speechless, staring intently at the brand-new baby. Stifling a sob, I wrapped my arms wound them both. My babies. My world. My everything.

Like any Mum with a new baby and an active toddler, life was chaos. I was trapped in that early cycle of sleep deprivation, constant breast-feeding and never-ending nappy changes, all the while trying to make sure the older one didn't feel pushed out. Damian was really helpful and involved for the first few weeks. He got up with Lewis in the mornings and helped with meals.

Daniel was less than a month old, when I got a tummy bug. It meant the hours I wasn't feeding him; I was throwing up. I was so weak I had to crawl to the bathroom.

Damian appeared with a cup of tea. 'There you go, babe.' He placed the cup on the bedside table and then kissed me on the head, looking down at baby Daniel.

'Please take him, I need to vomit again.'

I ran quickly to the en-suite bathroom and hurled into the bowl. I dragged myself up and was splashing my face with cold water, when I noticed Damian and Daniel in the mirror behind me.

'I'm going away to China for a week. It's free. Someone else has dropped out last minute, so Hattons have asked me. I'd be mad not to go. And it'd be good for business.'

My stomach turned. I was going to be sick again.

He'd made the bed and changed Daniel by the time I stumbled back through. 'Please don't go, Damian, if you don't have to,' I begged him. 'I'm exhausted. Daniel's awake most of the night, and I've got this awful tummy bug.'

'Sorry, babe, not my problem. Get your family to help. That's what they're there for.' Handing me the baby, he left the room, shrugging his shoulders.

I burst out crying the second he was gone. Holding baby Daniel, his tiny body pushed into me, as if feeling my pain.

'Mummy, I want breakfast now!' Lewis shouted from his bedroom.

***

In the weeks that followed Damian was going out more than ever. And when he wasn't out, he was on his phone. Never present.

'Why are you always making social plans, Damian? We've just had a baby, and you're never around. It's like you don't love me anymore.' A familiar pang of anxiety rose up my chest.

It was a Friday night, and as I piled washing into the machine, with Daniel on my shoulder and Lewis hanging round my ankles, Damian put on his new jacket. His expensive aftershave and slicked back hair assuring me he wasn't popping out for nappies.

'I don't see what all the fuss is about.' Damian sighed, rolling his eyes. 'It's no big deal. I have to work, I need a hobby, and I need to see my friends. Why should all that have to stop when we have another baby? I just don't get it. You should do it too. Go out whenever you want, Mandy. I'm not stopping you.'

He paced the floor for a few seconds before walking past me and up the stairs. I stood, with my nightie on, cradling Daniel in my arms and Lewis pulling on my leg. Catching his baby brother's eye, he made a face and giggled. I smiled, momentarily feeling lighter. Damian bounced down the stairs, humming a tune. Grabbing his phone, wallet, and car key, he headed off to band practice.

'Bye everyone!'

'Bye,' I whispered.

***

A couple of weeks later, the bubble of hope I'd somehow clung onto finally burst. I had dropped Lewis off at nursery and Daniel was tucked up and fast asleep for his morning nap. I put the kettle on and immediately noticed a mobile phone on the work top. My heart started to race. Picking the phone up, I tapped in the passcode. 'Invalid' popped up on the screen. I racked my tired brain. *What was the code again?* I had seen Damian tap his code in so many times, sat next to him on the sofa. I imitated his finger movements: 2-3-4-6. The phone immediately unlocked. I could almost hear my heart pounding in my chest. Pressing on text messages, I scrolled down a couple from work colleagues, a crass joke then a couple of messages from me then one from his friend, Robert. I opened it.

Is the ball and chain letting you go out tonight? It read. I clicked onto Damian's response. *It's not up to her the stupid cow, it's up to me!*

A wave of nausea washed over me.

Why don't you kick her out of the house and pack her off to one of your terraced houses in Rochdale? Ha! Ha! it read.

Don't tempt me mate! Damian had replied.

If the listener doesn't hear good about themselves, then the text reader may suffer the same fate, but nothing prepared me for the contempt in his exchanges. My heart was now racing faster and faster. Taking a deep breath, I steadied myself against the work top. *My husband despised me.*

***

It was May that year, baby Daniel was three months' old and finally beginning to sleep through the night. Lewis was nearly four. I had dropped him off at Mum's for a sleepover.

'Yeah! I'm going to Mama Bears!' Lewis yelled excitedly, when I told him that he was going away for a couple of nights.

It was a Wednesday afternoon. I sat on the sofa, biting the edges of my nails. It was a recently acquired habit. Daniel was kicking around on his play mat gurgling and giggling. I glanced at the clock, again. *He should be back soon.*

At last, I heard the key turning in the front door.

'Hi, babe!' Damian walked through into the lounge. 'You look nice.'

I was wearing more make-up than usual.

'Hello, little munchkin!' He bent down and picked up baby Daniel.

'We have to talk,' I told him.

Damian placed Daniel back down on the play mat and sat down on the couch opposite. 'Okay, babe, what is it?' He smiled, leaning back into the sofa.

I hesitated. I'd been planning this conversation for weeks, in my head, and now that it was here, I wasn't sure I could go through with it.

'Go on, spit it out.' Damian looked relaxed but sounded impatient.

'It's just not working, this, between us anymore.' I paused, feeling slightly out of breath. 'You're out all the time, you don't love me, and I've had enough.'

'I do love you, that's not true,' he said, slightly hesitating. 'But you're right, we're not working out, and we haven't been for the longest time. It's best for the boys if we end it now. Don't you think?'

I was nodding my head, but not really processing his words. Was this it? I had so much I wanted to tell him, but that was because I expected a fight or at the very least, a conversation. He agreed. We were on the same page. There was nothing left to say.

'I need to change Daniel,' I managed to mouth.

'You stay here, I'll do it.' Damian was on his feet with the baby in his arms before I could argue.

Like a schoolkid anxious to avoid a scolding, he was keen to bring our chat to a close. I'm not sure how long I sat there before they returned. Our years together flashing before me. The night we met… our first date… our first holiday… our first home… our first child… With every milestone, I'd forced myself to be hopeful. To believe that the next step would consolidate us as the committed couple we were, beneath his insecurities. And now, there was no-where left to place that hope. My marriage was over. My husband was relieved.

Damian returned with a laughing baby. 'I'll need access to the boys,' he said, placing Daniel back on his playmat.

'That goes without saying,' I said.

And yet, he was making me say it.

He was pacing around the lounge. Daniel was kicking his overhanging toys with a big smile on his face. I got up and walked over to him, bent down and kissed his soft cheek. He grabbed my hair and gurgled with delight.

'I'll see if I can move into Adam and Jeremy's for a bit until I get my own place.' Damian planned his single future, as I carefully prised my hair out of Daniel's tight grip. 'I'll make us both some tea,' he offered.

I nodded wordlessly. A couple of minutes later, Damian re-appeared holding a cup, scratching his head with his free hand. 'So, I was just thinking, Mandy, that we should divide the assets, and you have half of the money from the house.' He smiled at me.

'Sorry?' I rose to my feet. 'We don't need to start talking about settlements just yet, do we?'

I hadn't even mentioned divorce, we were less than an hour separated and here he was, selling our home... The man was desperate to end our marriage.

Damian moved out of our house and into Jeremy and Adam's. The transition was so smooth for him it was difficult to believe he hadn't planned it. He would see the boys at weekends, and a couple of evenings in the week. Slowly, we began to adapt to this new life.

***

The day before Lewis's fourth birthday I had just fed Daniel his last bottle and was getting him in his onesie. He grinned up at me and then shrieked with joy when he saw Lewis coming into his room.

Lewis walked over to his baby brother and passed him a teddy. 'Cuddle this in bed, Daniel,' he said.

'Lewis, how kind of you.' I reached down to give Lewis a hug. Daniel let out a little cry. 'Is someone getting jealous?' I scooped Daniel up, hugging him close.

Lewis smiled. *It was nice to see him smile.*

Once the boys were asleep, I went downstairs. Shortly after, Damian arrived. I had asked him to help with the preparations for Lewis' birthday. Sitting on the rug, bits of Sellotape on my hands, I wrapped the last of Lewis' presents whilst Damian sat on the sofa blowing up balloons. Furtively wiping away a tear, I felt so very sad. *We were a broken family. My precious boys were growing up in a broken*

51

home.

***

After the birthday party, Damian hung around in the kitchen for a bit.

'My living arrangements are changing,' he told me, 'I'm not staying with the guys anymore. I don't want to be on my own, so I'm going to be renting a flat with Mark.' He kept his eyes to the floor.

'What's happened with Jeremy and Adam?' I asked.

'They need their privacy.' He sniggered.

'What's that supposed to mean?' I hated Damian's innuendo.

'They've got a rent boy staying. Which is why I'm in a hotel.'

'A rent boy,' I repeated, unable to keep the disgust from my voice.

'They're grown adults, Mandy, they can do what they want. We're not all as uptight as you.'

That was unfair. Lots of people didn't approve of rent boys. That didn't make them repressed. Paying a young man for sex was hardly a morally neutral act.

'Who is this Mark?' I changed the subject. 'You've never mentioned him to me before.'

'He's a customer. Sales director for Mecada. Good guy. He has a girlfriend.'

'I don't see why you have to rent with him?' I continued. 'Wouldn't you want to get a place just for you and the boys?'

'You know I was telling you out of courtesy.' Damian's tone had completely changed. 'I'm moving in with Mark. That's where my sons will be staying. This conversation is over.' Picking up his jacket, he walked coolly out the door, leaving me shaken and confused. *Was he right? Could he just have anyone living with my boys? Was there nothing I could do to stop him?*

***

The boys would spend the night at the new flat almost every week, but it wasn't going very well. Lewis had started to become extremely distressed at the prospect of staying with Damian. He would scream and cry whenever his father came to collect him and his brother. Tonight was following this pattern.

'No, Mummy! No!" he shouted when Damian tried to pick him up. 'I want to stay with you!'

'It's okay sweetheart. Daddy will do some fun things with you, won't you, Daddy? I will see you tomorrow, that's just one sleep!" I tried to sound enthusiastic.

'Please, Mummy! I don't want to go with him!' He ran over to me, wrapping his arms around my legs looking up at me, pleading with his eyes. I could feel my chest tighten, as I forced my little boy to go with his dad. *He used to be like this when I first left him at nursery. Maybe Lewis was adapting and needed to adjust to the new situation? Maybe he just needed time…*

Time moved on and the situation became worse, not better. By now, the kids had been staying at Damian's new place almost six months. In their short life, it was the new normal, but Lewis continued to resist. There was the knock at the door when Damian was due to arrive. Lewis immediately darted off to his bedroom, and the battle to get him into the car would commence. I would cajole him and beg him and bribe him. I would alternate between firmness and kindness. I would get cross. It didn't matter how I approached it; the end game was the same. Lewis being dragged, kicking and screaming, to a house he didn't want to go to, to stay with someone he didn't trust. Every week, as I watched the car drive away, Lewis's howling ringing in my ears, I was consumed with the same sense of guilt and hopelessness.

This Saturday had been particularly gruelling. As soon as he'd woken up, Lewis had asked if his dad was taking them that evening, and from the moment I confirmed, the panic started. By the time he'd actually left, he'd been crying, on and off, most of the day. Watching his dad wrestle him from my arms, I could see the fear in his eyes, and I felt like I was betraying him. Waiting until nine pm when the boys were sure to be fast asleep, I picked up my phone and started ringing Damian. There was no answer. I tried again, fifteen minutes later, and still no answer, and fifteen minutes after that. Eventually, he called me back.

'What do you want, Mandy?' he barked into the phone.

'Damian, I've been thinking about how bad it is, at the moment, with Lewis, and how he gets so upset about going with you.' I rushed my words together, determined to say my piece. 'It must be really distressing for him, don't you think? Which is why we should maybe wait a while before Lewis stays at yours again. You have the boys all day but then bring them back at night. What do you think?'

For a few seconds, there was complete silence.

'Damian, are you there?' I asked.

He finally answered. 'You're a shocking parent!' he said. 'Shocking and stupid. *You* should be the one in charge. Not running around after Lewis. *We tell him* what is happening, not the other way around.'

I took a deep breath. 'Listen, Damian, I want Lewis to stay with his dad, as often as he wants to, but let's wait for Lewis to decide. He should be happy to go with you.'

'Don't mess with my time with my boys. It won't end well for you.' I could hear the menace in his voice then the line went silent.

The following night I was playing with Daniel before putting him to bed.

'Wow, look at you, clever boy!' I said.

Daniel was sitting up and clapping his hands. He was such a happy little baby. I picked him up, cuddling him close, pressing my cheek against him.

'You are irresistible!' I told my perfect baby.

Half an hour later after Daniel had fallen asleep, I was tucking Lewis into bed. Turning the lamp off I reached over to where he was lying and stroked his hair.

'I love you so much, Lewis.'

'I love you too, Mummy. So, so much.'

Keeping my tone light, I asked him, 'Why do you never want to stay at Daddy's?'

'Why should I want to stay with him?' he replied. He sounded exasperated like I'd asked him a silly question.

'Because he loves you and he's your Daddy'.

'I just don't like going there, Mummy,' he whispered.

'Why not, sweetheart?' I persisted. I knew I was pushing him, but I was desperate to help.

'I just don't,' he replied, turning over. 'I'm tired, I want to go to sleep, now.'

I sat on the edge of his bed caressing his face, as he drifted off to Dreamland.

Maybe he just preferred being with me? That wasn't uncommon, little kids often preferred staying at their mums.

A few weeks' later, I was in the kitchen preparing dinner. Lewis was meandering around on his swing car. Daniel was sat watching him and giggling. Lewis laughed back and upped the entertainment level making silly noises. I heard the phone ping with a new message. It was from Damian.

I want the boys to stay with me next weekend. This has gone on long enough. Lewis needs to know who's boss.

My fingers sweated as I slowly tapped out a reply

I'm not sending Lewis to yours until he is ready. It may only take a few weeks. You can see them as much as you like during the day and then just drop them off at bedtime.

I placed my phone onto the worktop, my heart racing faster, anticipating an angry response. I continued chopping onions. Sure enough, within a minute, the phone pinged.

I disagree. We tell him, not the other way around. You're not teaching him the right lessons in life. Life isn't easy. It's hard. You're going to regret this.

***

Christmas and New Year came and went. It was a cold, bright January morning when I went out to check the post. There was only one letter. I didn't recognise the sender. It looked official. Shivering, I returned to the warm house and opened it. It was from Manchester Family Court. *Family court? What was that?* I studied the document. It was an application made by applicant, Father (Damian) for overnight stays with the boys. *Why hadn't he told me he was going to do this? Why hadn't he waited for Lewis to be ready? Why was he forcing it through the court?* I would need to get a solicitor, it stated. I thought I was going to be sick. There was a hearing set for March.

I hadn't considered that the new year would consist of solicitor meetings, emails, phone calls and very expensive bills. It was a new world of recording and recalling information, double checking everything, as I prepared for the scrutiny of the legal system. Amy, my solicitor, had told me that things could go either way, that there was every chance the judge might compel Lewis to stay at Damian's. I nodded, as she explained this, but I didn't really take it in. With most of the education system and the caring system being child centred, there was no-way a court would force a kid's hand.

As I walked into the cold grey building for the hearing,

I immediately spotted Amy. She was stood with a large file in her hand. She held her other hand out to shake mine.

'Mandy, you look very smart,' she said, smiling.

After an hour, we were led into a dimly lit court room. Damian was already there, with his solicitor. In the raised chair ahead of us sat the clerk, dressed in a long black cloak. Damian's solicitor started the proceedings.

'The applicant father wishes to apply for overnight stays,' she began. 'The mother has been somewhat resistant to letting her sons stay with Mr Madford.'

'Why is that?' asked the clerk, peering over her glasses.

My solicitor stood up. 'My client has had a number of concerns, namely that her eldest son, Lewis, is getting upset about having to stay at his father's.'

After a few minutes of both our solicitors exchanging arguments, the clerk started to speak again. 'I am ordering that overnight visits take place once a week.' And with a swish of her cloak she left the room.

After the official order was made, I had no choice but to send the boys overnight, despite Lewis's continued distress. *I would have to try a different tactic.* For the next couple of months, I made every effort to make Lewis feel more comfortable around his dad. I invited Damian over for tea, made sure he attended nursery functions and arranged family days out. I didn't enjoy it. The court case had been the final nail in the coffin in any attempt at an amicable split, but I was determined to help Lewis.

The summer holidays were now over, and Lewis had now started his first year of reception. A few weeks into his first term, his teacher, Mrs Davies, approached me.

'Mandy, we're worried about Lewis. He isn't making progress the way we would expect him to. We are going to bring in the psychologist to assess him, if that's okay with you?' She smiled at me, sympathetically.

'Yes, anything that helps him,' I replied.

Why did my son need a psychologist? I was a full time, hands on mother, that had always been there. Why was that not enough?

The following week I had a meeting with the 'SENCO' (Special Educational Needs Coordinator). She was a matronly woman with a kind face and a gentle voice.

'Here are a number of activities I would like you to do with Lewis,' she said, handing me a list.

'Of course.'

The following day after school I sat down with Lewis to help him with his spelling. 'Well done, sweetheart!' I exclaimed, after a few minutes of teaching.

Lewis stood up with tears in his eyes. 'Mummy, I can't do anymore,' he spluttered, trying to get the words out. We had only learned two words.

Springing to my feet, I bent down and hugged my little boy. 'Don't get upset, you've done great!' I reassured him.

The activities set to help Lewis proved challenging. He didn't seem able to retain the information from day to the next. And I hated seeing him upset. I asked Damian to come over the following morning after I had dropped Lewis off at school.

'I've been doing all these tasks the SENCO gave me with Lewis, but it's just not making any difference,' I told him.

Damian took a slurp from his coffee, slammed it down on the work top and started walking out of the room. 'That's because you're a rubbish mother!' he shouted back to me from the hall.

That night I was running Lewis a bath. He was getting undressed when I noticed that he had little blisters on his bum.

'Sweetheart, you've got something on your bum, I'm just having a look, just stand still a minute.'

58

I inspected his skin. The blisters where nowhere else on his body. I could see they were around his anus too. The following morning, I booked an appointment with the doctor and managed to get a cancellation for the same day. After examining him, the doctor looked up at me. 'It's molluscum contagiosum. It's common in children. It can spread from child to child, sharing towels, that kind of thing.'

'Oh, he doesn't share towels with anyone,' I replied.

The doctor looked at me and smiled, deflecting my comment. 'They will disappear on their own in time. Just keep the area moisturised.'

That evening I told Damian about the diagnosis. 'It's called molluscum contagiosum,' I said.

Before I had got the words out Damian was replying, 'Sounds like something out of Harry Potter.'

***

It was now the summer holidays. We had activities arranged each week, as well as seeing family, meeting up with friends, and of course, seeing their father. And still Lewis cried every time Damian collected him. In fact, in spite of all my efforts to bring the family together, things were getting progressively worse. Lewis was wetting the bed, even though he'd been potty trained years. He was having nightmares. And he never wanted to leave my side.

Halfway through July, Damian took the boys to Devon for five days to stay with his parents. The contact arrangement order made by the family court included two holidays a year. He had made sure of that. The first morning after they left, I called to check in on them, especially Lewis, who had been inconsolable when his dad picked him up. I was about to hang up when Jean, Damian's mother, answered.

'Hello, Mandy,' she said coolly. She must have caller

ID.

'Hi, Jean. I'm calling to see how the boys are?'

'The boys are busy playing,' she snapped.

'Could I speak to them please?'

She paused. 'They're busy, Mandy. You're having fun though, aren't you boys?' Her voice softened a bit. 'I'll get them to call back later, okay?'

But they didn't call back. I rang that evening. There was no answer. Three days into their holiday I stopped trying to speak to them. There was no point. I dreaded that Lewis would simply think I'd abandoned him.

Summer turned into autumn and autumn turned into winter. I had my youngest with me full time, apart from the two mornings when little Daniel went to nursery. Drop off at nursery was very difficult, he would scream when they took him from me and beg to take him home.

'He'll take a while to settle,' the nursery worker tried to alleviate my concerns. But it wasn't just at nursery. Daniel was now screaming and crying just as much as Lewis whenever Damian came to collect them for the night.

'No, Mummy, I don't want to go with Daddy,' he would shout, every single time, without fail. 'I want to stay with my Mummy!'

I tried to talk to Damian, but it was like talking to a brick wall. He was completely indifferent to the boy's emotional state. 'But they always have a lovely time once they're at mine,' he'd counter, every time I queried his strategy.

As much as I wanted to believe him, I didn't. *If the boys were having such a blast, why were they always terrified to go?*

Somehow, in this state of constant conflict, every weekly visit as certain as the last to induce anger and panic, we bumbled along. I did everything I could to encourage them and reassure them, but my words fell on disbelieving ears. I'd pretty much given up trying to reason with Damian about any of it. The longer we spent apart, the more unreasonable he became. Mostly, I just got on with it. Two small boys meant they were always something to pick up or clean or someone that needed attention. The days blended into one long round of childcare and worry, and before I knew it, Lewis was starting his second year in school.

'Are you ready, Lewis?!' I shouted up the stairs, on the first day of term. There was no answer.

I walked upstairs, and found Lewis in his bedroom, still in his pyjamas, his clothes scattered across the bedroom floor.

'Lewis, why haven't you got dressed? You're going to be late for school!'

'I'm not going to school. I hate it!'

'Well you need to go and that's that,' I said. 'Come on, here, I'll help you with your clothes.'

The weeks that followed were one big struggle. I had to physically carry Lewis into school, sometimes, and walk away as he screamed my name, begging me not to leave. I had meetings with his teacher and the headteacher, Mrs Smith.

'We just don't know what to do with Lewis,' Mrs Smith concluded our chat, looking concerned. 'We've tried everything, and nothing seems to work.'

Excusing myself, I slipped into the nearest toilets and locking the door behind me, burst out crying. *If the experts couldn't help Lewis, what hope did he have?*

In the days after I saw his head, Lewis kicked up a massive fuss at school time. He was working himself into states that it was frightening to witness.

'Damian, you're going to have to come and help me with Lewis,' I said, when he answered the phone.

Twenty minutes later, Damian was over. Lewis got dressed.

'I wish he'd do that for me.' I sighed.

'You're too soft with him, that's your problem,' he replied.

'Come on Lewis, let's go,' I called, once he had finished breakfast. 'Damian. can you mind Daniel whilst I take Lewis to school?'

I pulled up in the car on the street outside the school.

'No, Mummy, No!' Lewis screamed, his fingers gripping the sides of his car seat, his little face white.

I looked at my distraught six-year-old son in the back of the car. *I can't do this anymore*!

***

'I'm home-schooling Lewis.' I announced to Mum the following day.

'Really, love? Do you think you would be able to manage that?' Mum couldn't keep the concern from her voice.

'I haven't got any choice, Mum. I can't make him go to school against his will, can I?'

'No,' Mum conceded.

That evening I broke the news to Damian.

'Well let's face it, Mandy, you'll be rubbish at teaching,' he sneered, 'but have it your way. I'll have Lewis on Thursdays, at least he might learn something then.'

I didn't bother arguing with him. He'd agreed and that was what mattered. Since the court case, I made sure he was included in all decisions.

The following Thursday, Damian returned with the boys, having spent the day with them, and invited himself for a cuppa. As I plugged the kettle in, he settled himself on the sofa. Lewis was stood close to me when he suddenly looked startled.

'Mummy! I've just wee'd out of my bum.'

Damian, who was leaning back into the sofa, arms over his head, piped up immediately, 'That'll be a wet fart.'

'What?' I asked.

Lewis dashed off to the bathroom and took off his underpants and went upstairs to get another pair. I picked up his underpants off the bathroom floor. They were wet and smelled of bleach, but they weren't soiled.

***

Within a month, I had enrolled Lewis at Forest School twice a week. It was run by teachers, and parents could leave their home educated children there for the day. It was essentially learning outdoors, with more freedom to participate in different activities. It sounded like the perfect answer to a kid who didn't like the confinement of school. It turned out he didn't like the outdoors either, least not if I wasn't by his side. He would freak out if I left and if I hung back to comfort him, he'd freak out even more when I tried to leave again. The pressure got too much and I stopped taking him. *What was wrong with my son?*

By the end of winter, I was now home-schooling Lewis full time, apart from Thursdays when he would go to Damian's. Daniel would go to playgroup a couple of mornings a week, and the rest of the time I would take the boys on home-schooling activities where the parents stay too.

One day, shortly after Damian had dropped Lewis off, I noticed that Lewis pulled a strange face.

'Are you okay, sweetheart?' I asked.

'Yes,' he replied.

A few minutes later he pulled the same expression, kind of like a grimace.

'You did it again, Lewis, are you okay?'

'I don't know what you mean, Mummy,' he replied.

It was after a few days that I realised Lewis had a tic.

***

'Do you fancy coming to Diggerland with me and the boys?' I asked Damian, on a sunny Friday May afternoon. I was always on the lookout for family events to include him in.

'Yeah, sure I'll come along,' he replied.

'It will be good for the boys to see us together and doing something fun!' I managed to keep my voice light.

On the drive up there, I felt Damian's fingers on my leg. I sat there, frozen, my eyes boring into his hand, willing him to move it. He didn't.

'I could make good money out of you,' he laughed.

'What did you just say?' I brushed his hand away

'I could,' he repeated, 'make real good money out of you.'

The rest of the journey passed in silence, with me looking out the window, trying hard to mask my tears. Why was I always searching for answers to why the boys feared their dad? Fact is, he was a nasty, horrible man.

***

Meanwhile, the house continued to not sell. It had been on the market over two years and whilst, initially, a few people seemed keen, now viewings had dwindled to a couple a quarter and no-one ever asked to return for a second visit. It was a beautiful house and I was grateful to have it but it wasn't ours. I was desperate to make the final break from Damian and move to a new home.

It was late summer, and Damian had just returned from having the boys for a few hours, one weekday. Lewis had spilled a drink in the car and was pulling his t-shirt off as he came into the house. He hated being wet. Immediately I noticed dark bruising across his shoulders and down his back.

'How on earth did Lewis get these bruises on his back?' I asked Damian.

He paused, looking straight at me. 'I was going to ask you the same thing.'

'No! No! No!' I raised my voice, 'He didn't get those when he was in my care.'

'Oh yeah, I remember now. He fell off a slide'.

'Really? That's not like you, sweetheart,' I said looking at Lewis.

He was such a careful boy.

'We can't all be helicopter parents like you, Mandy.' Damian meant it as an insult, but I was proud my children never suffered major accidents when I looked after them.

The following evening, I heard the sound of the gates opening, followed by car doors shutting and then gravel crunching. I opened the door. Damian was carrying Daniel who was fast asleep. Lewis was struggling to walk.

'Hi, Lewis, are you okay, sweetheart?' I asked, taking hold of his hand. 'Have you had a nice time?'

Lewis didn't answer. When we got into the hallway, he sat on the stairs, looking exhausted.

'You look tired,' I said. 'Come on, get you ready for bed.'

I helped Lewis upstairs and into his pyjamas.

'Mummy, can you come to bed now too?' he asked.

'Of course, I can,' I replied.

'Damian, can you get Daniel ready for bed?' I asked, running into his room to plant him a kiss on his soft cheek. He barely stirred.

'Wow, he's tired! You've tired them out, Damian! They're never this tired for me.'

Lewis was already curled up in my bed when I went back into my bedroom. I got into bed and stoked his hair. It was wet, and his face was hot.

'Goodnight, sweetheart,' I whispered.

Later on, when the entire household was sleeping, he woke me up.

'Mummy, cuddle me. Where's the dead baby?'

I wrapped my arms around him, as he shook and cried, and whispered calming platitudes in his ears. It was harder to calm my own mind, as I searched for answers as to why my boy was always in some state of trauma.

The following morning as I sat drinking my coffee, I looked over at Lewis, who was playing with his toys in the kitchen.

'Are you okay, sweetheart?' I asked.

There was no reply. I looked over at him, he was moving his cars around intently. *Was he autistic?*

***

It was a Friday evening, and I was getting ready to take the boys over to Damian's.

'I'll stay for tea?' I offered. As much as I'd grown to hate his company, I knew the only way to make the boys feel more at ease was to spend time together.

'I've only got pizza in, maybe another night?' Damian suggested.

'Pizza's great!' I replied. He didn't want me here anymore than I wanted to be here, but I wasn't doing it for him.

I sat on the sofa in between Lewis and Daniel whilst we ate our tea. Damian hung back in the kitchen. Mark, Damian's housemate, arrived back from work. He looked in the front room and smiled charmingly at me.

'Hi, Mandy.'

'Hi, Mark,' I replied.

He went into the kitchen briefly with Damian before going upstairs. I could hear the sound of the shower and music playing. Twenty minutes later, he appeared downstairs again going straight into the kitchen. I took our empty plates and cups into the sink. Damian was standing making a hot chocolate. Mark was standing beside him. They weren't speaking, but I got the impression I was interrupting something.

'Are you going to go then, Mandy?' Damian asked. *So, it wasn't just an impression.*

'Yes, I'll just go and sit with the boys for a few more minutes'

I sat down with the kids, and Lewis leaned into me.

'I'm going soon,' I said.

'No, Mummy, don't go!' Lewis begged.

'I can't stay here, there's no room for me to sleep,' I said, smiling.

'Please, Mummy, please!'

My insides twisted as my child's fear increased.

Lewis brought his knees up and started to rock then he grabbed a toy car and started to swirl it around his head. Daniel started to hit one of his toy cars off the floor. I hugged each son before saying my goodbyes.

After a restless night I collected the boys the following morning. They were irritable and tired. They were wearing some cast-off clothes that were too small that used to belong to Damian's nephews. I left loads of extra clothes; it made no sense. On the journey home the boy's fought with each other. Opening his window, Daniel threw his toy out. I screeched the car to a halt.

'Why did you do that?' I snapped. 'Now we have to go back and find it.'

'No, Mummy!' Daniel yelled. 'It's a horrible, disgusting car.'

Later that week, I took the boys to a local play area. Those ingenious spaces where kids can let off all their energy and the saviour of single mums everywhere.

'Wow! Look at you two climbing!' I enthused, tickling my boys through the netting.

Sitting down on a chair I had pulled up to the side I watched the boys playing. As I looked up, I noticed a woman who I had met though Damian. She was one of the band member's wives. Elaina Davey. She had three children, including a baby. Her icy blue eyes seemed to pause and stare at me. It felt significant, but it had been a while since we'd spoke, maybe she was trying to place me.

Treating myself to a latte, I spotted Elaina in the café and decided to say hello. I walked over to where she was sat.

'Hi, how are you all?' I asked.

'Oh, hi! I'm good, thanks, how are you?'

We exchanged pleasantries and chatted about the baby.

'Is your youngest walking yet?" she asked.

'I should hope so.' I smiled, puzzled. 'He's three and a half!'

'Is he indeed?' she replied. 'They grow up so fast.'

Our brief conversation over, I walked back to check in on the boys. There was something not quite right about our exchange, but I couldn't put my finger on it. Glancing around, trying to locate Lewis and Daniel, I realised they'd moved. I climbed through the play area and found them in the dance room.

'Hi, guys, are you okay?' I called over to Lewis.

'Yes, Mummy, we're playing with our friends!' Lewis yelled back.

I looked to see who he meant. It was Liam and Alanna. Elaina's children. My earlier discomfort was starting to make sense. *Why was she trying to make out that she hadn't seen my sons for years? I had only recently seen a photograph on Damian's phone, taken with her and Damian and the boys and her children.*

***

Finally, a couple in their sixties made a reasonable offer on the house. Hanging up on the estate agent I realised I was crying. We had been waiting for this for so long that I had started to doubt anyone would ever buy it. It had been over three years since we put the house on the market in June 2011. And now in July 2014, we could finally add a "Sold" to the sign outside.

I immediately started looking at houses near to my family. I wanted to live in the next village along. It was quiet with a few shops, and a lovely park and was close to my family and to the countryside. After I had viewed a handful of houses, I rang Mum one morning.

'I've just seen a house I like the look of in Littleborough. Could you nip over and have a quick look for me?'

'Yes of course, love,' she replied.

That afternoon we both drove over to see it. The village was the nicest in the area nestled just below the hills. It had a rural feel to it, but it also had its own high street with cafes, shops and a local school. Best of all there was a scenic park on the other side of the road opposite the entrance to the cul-de-sac where the 1960s semi-detached house lay on a quiet, secluded row of houses. It had front and back gardens, with a little path leading up to the front door.

'Hi, you must be Mandy.' A friendly looking lady answered the door and gave us both a warm smile.

'Please come in. Have a look around, on your own, if you like,' she offered.

Taking off our shoes, I replied, 'Yes, please.'

It had a spacious bright lounge with adjoining dining room, large windows, a decent sized hallway and a small old-fashioned kitchen, complete with a new boiler and central heating. Upstairs there were three decent sized bedrooms and a dated but good-sized bathroom. There would be room for a separate shower. It had been freshly painted and had brand-new carpets throughout. Roaming from room to room, imaging the colours I would paint it and the places I'd hang pictures. I could feel myself falling in love with its potential. *It was perfect.* After five minutes of looking around the cosy three bed semi I had decided what offer I was going to put in.

Within a week I was packing to leave. I had asked Damian to come over and pick up the last of his stuff. He arrived mid-morning and knocked on the door of Lewis's bedroom. Mum had taken both the kids, and I was up to my elbows in soft toys and board games.

'Here,' he said, handing me a laptop.

'What's that for? We have the main computer,' I asked, barely looking up. I was busy sorting stuff that mattered, from stuff they wouldn't notice if I threw it away. It was a fine line. If the teddy they hadn't played with in six months was disposed of, they might suddenly remember tomorrow he was their favourite toy.

'You won't have the room for the desk and this big computer in your house,' Damian replied. 'You may as well get rid of it. I'll take it today.'

'It's still quite new though, we could sell it?' I offered.

'It wouldn't be worth it!' he snapped. Damian busied himself disconnecting the computer.

'Hold on a minute,' I said, 'I've got photographs and things on there I want to keep.'

Damian sighed, scratching his head. 'Okay, just give me ten minutes. I'll nip home and get you some discs to copy them on'

'It's a lot of messing around for you, Damian, aren't you flying out to Holland first thing? I'll get some discs tomorrow and take it to the recycling at the weekend,' I said.

'I said I'd do it, now, didn't I?' Damian snapped again.

I didn't want to argue with him, but I'd actually asked him over to help, and the only thing he seemed interested in doing was making sure we got rid of his computer.

***

Contracts exchanged; the sale completed at the end of October 2014. After an exhausting few days, I had moved most of our things in and I was excited to show the boys around.

'What do you think of your new house then?' I asked them both.

'I like it, Mummy' Lewis shrieked, jumping off the freshly made bed in his room.

'Me too!' Daniel chirped in.

We were still waiting on our dining room table so that night we ate a picnic on the floor.

I sat on the carpet against the wall, with my arms around each of my sons. *This would be the start of a new chapter. Things would get better from now.*

Mum came over the day after we moved. 'It's so good to have you nearby,' she said smiling.

'I know, it's wonderful! Do you want a cup of tea?' I asked.

'Yes, please, love,' she replied.

'I've been quite productive,' I said, putting the kettle on. 'I've enrolled Daniel at a local nursery for a couple of days. And I think I've found a decent tutor for Lewis to help out once a week.' I handed her a leaflet. Mum read through it.

'That sounds great, Mandy.'

'And I've already hooked up with the local home ed groups. I'm taking Lewis to a sports session in the morning.' I grinned.

The following morning, during our first sports class, I was sat with the other mums. and the children were running around playing with footballs. One of the other kids was joking around being a bit rough and tumble. Suddenly, Lewis burst out crying. Rushing over to him I put an arm around him.

'It's okay. sweetheart, the little boy was only playing.'

That evening, Naomi and Mum had come over for dinner. We sat around the newly arrived table eating pasta and salad.

'I was thinking about taking Lewis to karate,' Naomi suggested. 'It could help with his confidence?'

Lewis seemed excited at the prospect. He was very close to his aunt.

So, my sister enrolled them both into a beginner's class.

The first couple of sessions went okay. After his third-class Naomi took me aside. 'He's finding it difficult to take instructions and makes random erratic noises.'

'Does he?' I asked, sighing.

'The instructor asked if there was anything wrong with Lewis, like autism. I said no. You don't think he is autistic, do you Mandy?'

'I've already looked into that,' I told her. 'He doesn't tick many of the boxes. The school didn't think he needed testing.'

'I don't know what to do, Naomi,' I confided. 'I've tried every remedy under the sun. Clean, healthy organic food, reflexology for children, homeopathic medicine, Bach's flower remedies. I home school him. I make sure he gets lots of exercise. I'm always reassuring him and telling him how loved he is, and none of it makes a difference. What's wrong with him?'

I hadn't meant to get upset, but tears streamed down my face. They say you are only as happy as your least happy child, and my eldest son hadn't seemed happy in years.

Four

We were well settled into our new home and preparing for our first Christmas. Despite the upheaval I had a real sense of hope about our move. This house was ours, and our financial dependence on Damian was severed. It was yet another new start, but I had managed to convince myself it was the one that counted. Neither boy was exactly stable, but with our change of circumstances there was the hope that it was only a matter of time.

We quickly developed a daily routine that gave the boys ample free time but also tended to their educational needs. They still woke early so they watched some morning tv before we all helped with breakfast. After eating, we'd have some outside play, followed by the first of four short educational activities. Acutely aware of Lewis's anxiety around learning, the plan was to aim for little and often. We had some success with the model, but with Lewis it often felt like one step forward, two steps back.

It was an early winter's Saturday morning, which meant no school lessons and lounging around. I was looking forward to taking Lewis 'Horse Whispering'. I tried everything already that year, healing foods, homeopathy, reflexology, and now I was giving horse whispering a go. Whatever that was. Lewis had a special bond with animals, maybe this would help my son.

I felt a chill in the air hit me as I opened the front door.

'Hi.' Damian walked into the hallway. 'You okay? Where are they then?'

He headed into the spacious living room where the boys were playing, pausing to take off his jacket.

'Why don't you show Daddy your new bedroom before you go?' I suggested.

'Wow, what a cool bedroom!' Damian enthused.

'We got the biggest bedroom!' Lewis announced proudly.

'My willy's sore,' Daniel suddenly spoke out of nowhere.

'You'll have to watch out for his foreskin getting tight,' Damian said, yawning.

I nodded, not really sure what he was talking about.

'So, you're going to go horse whispering today I hear Lewis?' Damian asked.

'Yes, Mummy can we go now?' Lewis asked, looking at me.

'Just you and me then Daniel.' Damian said, reaching a hand towards our youngest son.

'No, Mummy!' Daniel shouted, running into my bedroom.

'Ah, come on you, come with Daddy.' Damian said, going after him and carrying him downstairs.

'Have fun, Lewis,' he said, leaving the house as I reached out to touch my youngest son's outstretched hand.

'Love you, sweetheart!' I shouted after Daniel. 'Damian, I'll drop Lewis off at yours for five.'

After a heart-warming couple of hours with Lewis getting to know 'Sally' the horse and learning how to lead her and read her body language, we decided to buy some food from the health food shop nearby.

'We've got a bit of time to kill.' I said to Mum.

'Mummy, do I still have to go to Daddy's?' Lewis asked.

'Yes, it'll only be for a couple of hours, and then he'll drop you off again.' I tried to sound enthusiastic.

We dropped Mum off and said our goodbyes, but as I drove away in the car, I realised that I had forgot to check if Damian was at home, as we were arriving early. *Maybe they'd be at the park?* Ten minutes later it was just after four o-clock when I pulled up outside the painted white terraced house. I noticed the downstairs curtains were closed. Taking my phone out of my handbag, I started to ring Damian. There was no answer.

'Come on, Lewis, let's go and knock,' I said.

We stood outside of the house knocking on the door for about five minutes before he answered, smiling.

'How was it, Lewis?' he asked.

Walking through into the lounge, I immediately saw Daniel sat on the black leather sofa, staring straight at the film on the television, *Ice Age*. He hadn't noticed me and Lewis walk in.

'Hi, Daniel' I said.

He didn't turn around.

'I've never seen you glued to a film like this!'

He still didn't make eye contact. He sat, totally still, staring at the screen.

'Mum, can I not just come home with you?' Lewis asked again.

'Come and watch *Ice Age* with us,' said Damian 'Your brother's favourite, he's been glued to it,' he laughed.

But on the drive home, I couldn't shake off the strange feeling that something wasn't right.

A few days later, on Tuesday 2nd December 2014, I awoke to the sound of Lewis getting out of bed.

'Morning, love.'

'Hi, Mummy.'

'Here, put this on.' I hugged him close before handing him his soft, fluffy dressing gown.

Once both boys were up and dressed and had polished off some pancakes with maple syrup, I sat down them down at the dining table.

'Let's do some little words,' I suggested. 'Then you can play for a bit.'

Daniel took a felt tip pen and began to draw circles on the paper. 'That's my name,' he said proudly.

'Beautiful!' I smiled. And your writing is beautiful too, Lewis,' I said, looking over at my eldest, who was struggling to hold his pen. 'Let's try with some two letter words, shall we?' I was conscious of keeping my tone upbeat.

Lewis looked down at the paper. 'I can't!' He flung his pencil across the room.

'Of course, you can. How do you write the word "at"?' I asked.

Lewis' eyes filled up with tears.

His trauma was interrupted by a knock at the door. Climbing off their chairs, both boys went to look out of the window.

'It's Mama Bear!' Daniel squealed in delight. Lewis' response was more muted, but I could tell he was pleased.

'My client cancelled so thought I'd come over.' Mum beamed at her grandsons, giving each a hug and kiss. 'What's the matter, sweetheart?' she asked Lewis.

'I can't write.'

Mum looked at me. I shrugged my shoulders.

'It's okay, Lewis, we'll come back to it later,' I told him, gathering up the pages and slipping them into their learning folders.

'Do you want to come back to my house, Lewis?' Mum asked.

'Yes, Mama Bear!' He ran to grab his coat off the hanger in the hall.

'Thanks, Mum,' I mouthed as Lewis yanked her hand and pulled her out the front door.

'Just you and me, eh?' I smiled at Daniel. 'Fancy going to a cafe for some tasty treats?'

'Yes, please, Mummy!' he shouted, bouncing up and down in excitement.

It was good to have just me and him time. Yet another advantage to having Mum so close. Wrapping us both up snugly, I felt a rush of gratitude for where we all were in the world. Our local café was packed. There were still a few weeks of shopping to go, but by the look of the present bags piled around the seats, not much left to buy. Daniel and I found a place in the corner, and he set to work colouring the free picture mat, whilst I ordered for us both. Hot chocolates drank and brownies devoured, we strolled through the streets taking in the twinkly fairy lights and laughing Santas in the shop windows. By the time we got back to our house we were both exhausted, and Daniel climbed onto to the sofa to watch cartoons, whilst I set about making us fish fingers and mashed potatoes.

I smiled as I looked at him sitting on the sofa holding his favourite teddy, intently watching the Peter Rabbit show. My phone rang.

'Hi, Mum,' I answered, walking upstairs to escape the blaring television.

'Hi, Mandy.'

There was a long pause.

Everything is Going to Be Okay

'Are you there, Mum?'

Eventually, she spoke, 'Lewis has just told me that his daddy touches him on his bottom and willy when he plays on the Xbox.'

I didn't respond. I wasn't sure what she was saying.

'Mandy?' Mum's voice sounded scared.

'What do you mean?' I asked. *I must have misheard her.*

'Lewis just told me his Daddy touches him. He was just sitting stroking the cats in your old bedroom when he told me. He just told me just before I called you.'

I gasped. I was standing in my bedroom my back against the warm radiator. I walked to my bedroom door and stood in the doorframe for a moment. I heard a shriek. *Did that come out of my mouth?* Mum started to speak again. 'And then he said that "I don't mind though…" and that "Daddy said that Granddad Bill did the same to him when he was a little boy and he gave him sweets…"'

Time seemed to stand still. I don't remember anything else about that night.

***

The following days were a blur. Day blended into night and night blended into one long nightmare. I awoke each morning with the same sick feeling. *Was it all a horrible dream?* I looked at the sleeping boy at the side of me and wanted to sob and scream.

'We need to retain a level of normality, for the boy's sakes,' Mum said, a few days later.

I nodded in agreement, even though I knew nothing would ever be normal again.

'Let's go and choose a Christmas tree,' Mum suggested.

That afternoon we headed out to the Garden Centre. Stacks of trees were lined up in the aisles. The scent of pine filled the cold air. The boys smiled as they gazed at the sparkly lights hanging overhead.

'How about this one, boys?' Naomi pulled out a plump tree.

'Yes, I like it!' Lewis gave her two thumbs up.

Daniel was more interested in the decorations. 'Can I have this, Mummy?' he asked, handing me a big, red sparkly bauble.

'Of course, you can, love.'

Once home we decorated the tree until it was lit up and covered with colour and tinsel. The television blared out, and the boys were sat on the settee eating supper. My phone pinged. It was a text message from Damian.

I'll come for the boys at 5pm tomorrow, it read. Dropping the phone onto the sofa I could feel my head spinning. *I would have to think of an excuse.*

'Right, I think it's your bedtime, sweetheart,' Naomi said, taking hold of Daniel's hand. 'Let's go and choose you a book.'

Half an hour later, Daniel was fast asleep.

Lewis and I lay sprawled on the couch, flicking through one of his books.

'Lewis, it's your bedtime, now,' I told him, pulling myself up.

Lewis hesitated. He hugged his knees to his chest. 'I have more stuff to tell you about Daddy,' he said.

As he spoke, his eyes searched for mine. Turning off the television, I pushed baubles and tinsel out of the way and sat down on the carpet.

'Come, sit here with me.' I squeezed his hand gently.

'Daddy said every day, "If you tell anyone then you'll never see Mummy again", and I love you so much, that's why I didn't say anything.' Lewis looked straight at me. 'Mummy, will I still be able to carry on seeing you?'

I pulled him into my chest and stroked his hair with my hands. Blinking back tears, I promised him, 'Of course you will sweetheart. You're safe now.'

'I was so scared because I love you so much, Mummy. I had no one to tell, except Daddy, and Daddy said, "Get over it!"' His imitation of Damian was spot on.

He leaned his body into mine, and I hugged him hard.

'You're safe now, though. You brave, brave boy.'

We sat there for the longest time with me rocking him back and forth, whispering words.

How could I have not known? How could I have been so blind that I didn't see the signs? Why didn't I put up hidden cameras? What could I do to help my son?

I scanned through the Amazon app on my phone, looking for a book that would help my traumatized son. I found one called *The Right Touch*. It had been recommended by top child psychologists.

***

'We need to go to the police,' Naomi said. She handed me a cup of tea.

'I know.' I couldn't bear to think about it, but I knew I had to do it.

'I've been thinking,' Naomi continued. 'He gave you his old laptop, remember?'

'Yeah, I've been using it for months now. Do you think there will be something on it?'

'I think it's worth checking out,' Naomi replied.

I'd already started to log on. I noticed a small Gmail icon in the corner, with "Damian Madford" on it. I clicked onto the icon. A window popped up on the screen with Damian's emails. My eyes flicked down the list. It was mainly customers in the carpet trade. There was a calendar entry for once a fortnight every Saturday. It read "Office - boys."

'I can see Damian's emails,' I called to Naomi who was making us both a sandwich in the kitchen. She abandoned our snack and sat down on the couch beside me.

'Okay, you might be able to see his search history,' Naomi took the laptop from me and started to scroll.

'There's about eighteen months of history here Mandy. He's accessed a lot of paedophile news stories, look.'

'*Young teen gang bangs…Rent boys…*and look, he goes onto a porn site straight after each story.'

'*Teen escorts in Manchester,*' she continued to read. '*Smothered.*'

'What in God's name is *"Smothered"*?' I asked.

Naomi shook her head. 'You don't want to know, Mandy.'

She was right, I didn't want to know any of this but what choice did I have?

'What's this postcode?' Naomi was continuing to read through his emails. 'Write this down OL11, he goes to this address all the time.'

I typed the code into my phone. 'Found it,' I replied. 'It's in Heywood.'

'I'll have a drive over there tonight, check it out.' Naomi said.

'Look there's another postcode.'

'That's his office,' I said.

'Why would he put the postcode in for his office?'

'There's a pattern,' Naomi said. 'Once a fortnight on a Saturday he put the postcode into his phone. And he goes to the address in Heywood nearly every day, sometimes twice in the same day.

'Okay, I think I've worked out what he's doing. He's sending the postcode to other people. It's a meeting place.'

'Right, I'll go look at that office space and let you know what I find, and you get some rest.'

'I'm going to need it if I'm calling the police tomorrow,

eh?' My eyes filled with tears.

'Don't worry, Mandy.' Naomi placed her arm around my shoulder. 'The police are trained to deal with these situations. They'll help us all make sense of this. It will be a weight off once you've spoke to them.'

***

The following morning, I dropped the boys off at Naomi's and drove back home. Dialling the number slowly, I could feel my hands shake.

'Hello, Greater Manchester Police. How can we help?' a female answered.

'I'd like to report a crime.' My voice was barely audible.

'Can you speak up, please?' the woman asked.

I repeated my request.

'Okay, can you give me the details please?'

'My eldest son, Lewis, is being sexually abused by his father, Damian Madford.'

Later that afternoon there was a knock at the door. I answered and saw two men.

'Hello, are you Amanda?'

'Yes,' I croaked.

'I'm DC Colin Webster, and this is Keith Dawson from social services.'

DC Webster was a slightly overweight man in a too tight uniform that caused him to perspire, leaving a glistening effect on his face. His colleague Keith Dawson was taller and thinner and cleaner. I invited them both in.

'I'm here to take a statement from you, and Keith is taking some notes for his report.'

I nodded.

'Okay, so, Amanda, if you could just start from when your son, Lewis, disclosed.'

I began at the point where Mum had told me. The words didn't seem to come from my mouth. I spoke for about ten minutes whilst both men took notes. When I finished, we all sat in silence for a couple of minutes before DC Webster spoke.

'Thanks, Amanda. I am going to arrange for your son to be questioned tomorrow, okay?'

'I guess so,' I replied.

'I'll go and arrange it now, Amanda, and call you back later.' DC Webster was making his way towards the door. Keith Dawson quickly packed away his laptop and followed. As they drove away, I sat in my kitchen and sobbed.

***

The familiar pang of dread washed over me as I came out of my slumber. Pulling the duvet over my head, I tried to escape back into sleep. It was useless. After a few minutes I got up, stepped into my slippers, pulled on my dressing gown and headed downstairs to make a cup of strong tea. Sipping my hot tea, I planned on how I would tell Lewis. Minutes later, I heard footsteps coming down the stairs.

'Mummy?' Lewis sounded worried.

'I'm in the kitchen, love,' I called to him.

He walked through the door, and I gathered him in my arms.

'Morning sweetheart,' I said, inhaling the scent of his hair.

'Mummy, what are we doing today?' he asked.

'How about we make Christmas decorations?'

'Yes!' Lewis clapped his hands together.

Art stuff was a great leveller, it didn't make him feel desperate like academic stuff did.

'Before we go get everything, remember how I said I spoke to the police yesterday?' I chose my words carefully.

His eyes clouded over. 'Yes,' he whispered.

'Well they want to speak to you about the things you

told us that Daddy did.'

I watched him consider what I was saying before replying. 'Okay, Mummy, I'll talk to them. Will they protect me then?'

'Yes, of course, sweetheart, they will. They're the good guys.'

I glanced outside, watching the trees swaying around in the wind against the grey sky.

Later that morning we pulled up outside a big building with the sign, Greater Manchester Police. It had recently been treated to some kind of paint job that did little to make it more inviting. I gave Lewis some change and he ran off to put it in a meter.

'Look, Mummy, there's Aunty Nonie,' Daniel said, waving at his aunty who was walking across the car park.

Naomi opened Daniel's car door and helped him out of his car seat.

'Hi Daniel.'

Mum and James appeared. Mum rushed over to Lewis. 'How's my brave boy?'

'I'm okay,' Lewis said solemnly.

Naomi called me to one side and whispered, 'James and I drove over to that house in Heywood on Damian's searches. It stands out. It's a right mess, really rough.'

'Hopefully, the police will search it,' I whispered back.

Naomi took Daniel's hand. 'Let's go and hang out with Uncle James,' she told him.

Meanwhile Mum and I each took one of Lewis' hands, and we walked into the small reception of the police station.

'Hello, can I help?' the officer behind the desk asked.

'I'm Amanda Taylor. My son Lewis is being interviewed.' I squeezed Lewis' hand gently.

'Okay, take a seat and someone will be with you

shortly.'

It was a busy station, and officers milled about as we sat waiting. Mum kept Lewis occupied with a game of I Spy, whilst I silently prayed. At last a woman appeared in the doorway opposite.

'Hi, Amanda. I'm DC Sawyer, I'm here to interview Lewis.'

She was about forty, quite attractive and looked friendly. I felt relieved. She seemed like someone Lewis might relate to.

'Hi,' I replied, standing up with Lewis who had my hand in a tight grip.

DC Sawyer looked down at Lewis. 'Hi, Lewis. I'm going to ask you some questions, okay? But I'm not here to be your friend.'

Panic rose in Lewis' face

Why would she say that to him?

DC Sawyer led us through an underground corridor past a maze of disused cells. Eventually we arrived into the interviewing area. It consisted of several rooms. A tiny waiting room, a couple of interviewing rooms and a viewing room with cameras.

'This is the room where I will be with Lewis,' she explained.

'Can I come too?' I asked. Lewis had graduated from squeezing my hand to digging his nails into me.

'I'm afraid not. It's policy,' DC Sawyer responded. 'I'm sorry.'

She didn't sound it.

We looked round the room. It was sparce, containing a couple of blue sofas, a table, and a camera set up in the corner. There was no window.

'And this is the observation room.' She opened the next door along. Another policeman and a social worker were already seated, waiting for Lewis' interview to start.

'Hi, Lewis, we will be watching your interview and taking some notes.' The policeman smiled at him.

'Will Mummy be in here too?' Lewis asked. I could hear the hope in his voice.

'No, but she will be in the waiting room just over there, okay?'

Lewis looked nervous.

'You'll be okay, sweetheart,' I wrapped my arms around him and hugged him hard.

'We'll just be over there, and you can have a hot chocolate when you've finished,' Mum added.

'Why did she say that thing about not being his friend?' I asked as soon as Mum and I were alone.

'I don't know, love, but it's no way to speak to a traumatised child.'

After about an hour, DC Sawyer popped her head around the door. 'He's just having a break. I gave him a hot chocolate.'

She gave us both a smile.

I sighed. *Why was it taking so long?*

Half an hour later, Lewis and DC Sawyer both appeared at the door.

I reached out my arms, and Lewis collapsed into them.

'Lewis did well, didn't you?' DC Sawyer said. 'He told me some things about Daddy touching him on the willy and bum. Lewis, why don't you get Grandma a drink while I have a chat with Mummy?' she said.

When she was satisfied Lewis was out of earshot, she told me, 'we will be sending someone to arrest Mr Madford later today.'

The car journey home was exhausting with Lewis shooting at Daniel for no reason and continually kicking the back of my seat.

'Stop it!' I eventually snapped only for him to burst out crying. I pulled the car over, climbed in the back and held my traumatised child. 'It's okay, darling, the worst is over. Now it's Daddy's turn to answer questions; nobody will ask you any more.'

'Will they lock him up?' Lewis asked when his tears had subsided.

'They will, darling, for a very long time.'

We arrived home, had lunch and the boys were playing in their bedroom. James and Naomi had come back to ours, and we were sitting in the lounge drinking coffee. Damian had been texting all afternoon. He wanted to see the boys, and he wanted to know why he hadn't seen them. His messages were getting increasingly abusive. I read the last one out loud.

You really are the lowest piece of shit. If you don't let me see the boys, I will take further steps which will be detrimental for everybody.

'He could turn up,' James said what we were all thinking. 'Why don't we just go out?'

'We could go to the Top Brink, get some food? It's out of the way,' Naomi suggested.

'Let's do it. I'll get my bag, you get the boys,' I told them.

I couldn't face it if he showed up, and I was worried what seeing him might do to Lewis.

Half an hour later we pulled up outside of Top Brink. It was a family run restaurant on the top of a hill, twenty miles from home. As I walked into the pub, I was transported back to my own childhood. We had spent many a happy Sunday teatime here.

The low ceilings had beams, and Naomi warned James, our tallest diner, to be careful. We had just been handed the menus when my phone started ringing. It was a withheld number.

'Hello,' I answered.

'Hi, Amanda, it's Colin Webster. We've arrested Damian Madford. I'll give you an update tomorrow.'

Slipping my phone back into my pocket, I gave James and Naomi a knowing look and said a silent prayer of thanks.

The car journey home was quite mellow. The boys had both had bowls of pasta and garlic bread and, spaced out on carbs, were half dozing in the back, staring out separate windows.

'I have to work and Daddy's the teacher,' Daniel said, suddenly, eyes wide open.

'What do you mean, sweetheart?' I asked.

'Anyway, I'm not telling anyone 'cos the police will get me…' he continued.

'What do you mean, darling?' I asked again.

'Anyway, can we have some cereal later?'

I watched Daniel's face in the rear-view mirror. He was grinning as he reeled off his favourites, 'Coca Pops, Cheerios, Rice Krispies. What's yours, Mum?'

'Cornflakes, every time,' I answered.

I could barely sleep that night. The echo of Daniel's words in the car kept ringing through my ears.

"Anyway, I'm not telling anyone 'cos the police will get me."

After making the boys breakfast, I carried a cup of tea upstairs. I checked my phone for the twentieth time. *I still hadn't heard anything.* I scrolled through my contacts until I found the number.

'Hello, DC Webster,' I spoke sharply, 'it's Amanda Taylor. I'm calling because I haven't heard from you...'

'Oh, yes,' he interrupted, 'we released Damian, pending investigation. I was going to call around to see you late to give you more of an update. Is that okay?'

I must have said yes before I dropped the phone. *He*

was out! He was out! How could that happen. They only arrested him yesterday. How could they have released him already? The rest of the morning was a blur of checking my phone and checking out the window. As soon as his car came into sight I was at the front door. I watched his large frame approaching through the frosted glass.

'Hi, Amanda,' he said,

'Please come in.' Holding the door open I was conscious my hand had a slight tremor.

DC Webster walked through the lounge and sat down on the sofa opposite. 'Okay, so, as you are aware, I questioned Mr. Madford yesterday evening. He was bailed. During the investigation he's not allowed to contact you or the boys, and he can't be alone with any children under the age of sixteen.' He paused, looking straight at me. 'So, I'm going to be honest here. Damian didn't look like a paedophile. His house was immaculate, and he was very helpful with the enquiries.' He sat back into the sofa like he was in his own home.

"He didn't look like a paedophile." What does that even mean? 'But, what about what Lewis said?' I croaked.

'Well, children can say these things when parents separate,' he responded.

'We separated three years ago.' *Keep the emotion out of your voice!*

'Well he's an impeccable character that would stand up well in court.' He continued, 'Fathers have rights, you know. I asked him if he was attracted to children and he said "no".'

What did you expect him to say? 'What about the information on his laptops?' I asked.

'We'll have a look at his laptop.'

'He has two laptops,' I retorted. *Don't snap! Don't let him make you angry!* 'Did you look into the address in Heywood?'

My voice grew quieter.

'Yes, I did. It's a known property,' he replied.

'Known, known for what?' I asked.

'It's known to the police.' Webster stood up, as if he was intending to go.

'What's it known for?' *I needed answers.*

'I'm not allowed to give you that information.' He had slipped his notepad back into his pocket.

'But what if it's known for child abuse?' *Surely, he could see how relevant that would be!*

'It wouldn't matter if they were convicted paedophiles.'

'I don't understand,' I confided, all pretence of strong woman having dissipated.

He looked me up and down before glancing around the room. 'Nice house by the way.'

'Thanks,' I muttered, but I knew he hadn't meant it as a compliment.

'You remind me of my ex-wife.' He gave me a sly smile.

'What did you say?' *Had I heard him, right?*

He paused at the door, grinned again and reiterated, 'Yeah, you're just like her.'

The rest of the night I kept myself busy. I sorted out the boy's book shelves and re-organised their wardrobe. I was too agitated to sit and play with them, so I shoved an Octonauts DVD on a loop and focused on housework. We had tea in front of the telly, and then Lewis chilled with his iPad whilst I bathed Daniel and put him down.

'Time for bed,' I called to Lewis.

I hadn't stopped since Webster left, like if I allowed my mind to think about what he had said, it would explode.

Lewis was easier to get ready for bed than Daniel, less wriggly, and as we lay side by side and he drifted off, I finally confronted my thoughts about the day. Madford didn't look like a paedo, and I did look like the arresting officer's ex-wife, and neither of those facts boded well.

'Mummy, are you still awake?' Lewis nudged me.

'I am, darling,' I replied.

'Why did it have to happen to me, Mummy?' His voice was slightly louder than a whisper.

'I'm so sorry, sweetheart. It should never have happened to you.' I fought back tears.

'Why did you marry him, Mummy? Why didn't you marry someone else?'

'I wish I had married a nice man, Lewis; I really do.' I took his hand and held it gently.

'He did bad things to me, Mummy, horrible things.' He cuddled into my chest.

'What did he do to you?' I asked.

'He did horrible things with his body to my body, and when he put his willy in my bum, it really, really hurt Mummy.'

His voice seemed to pierce through the dark night straight into my heart as hugged into me. Eventually, his breathing slowed down. I pulled my aching arm from underneath him, and he rolled over. I slowly climbed off the bed and pulled the duvet over him. I paused at the door to look at my sleeping son.

'God, please protect my little one,' I whispered before gently closing the door, falling on my knees on the landing in a silent prayer. I prayed as I wiped the tears away that were streaming down my cheeks. I headed downstairs, curled up on the sofa and began having flashbacks. *Lewis must have just been raped by his father when he told me he'd wee'd out of his bum…the poor performance at school… his separation anxiety…the immense fear at going with Damian…. the deterioration of his happiness… his lack of joy…the night sweats…curling up into a foetal position all the time…*

Every unexplained incident began to make sense. The

final piece of a strange and very large jigsaw puzzle had just been put into place. And I was jolted awake out of a long, deep sleep.

***

The night after followed the same pattern. With the lights out, and Daniel fast asleep, Lewis had more to tell me. Before he even spoke, I sensed he was about to.

'Mummy, some of Daddy's friends touched me. It was in a meadow near their house and in a park, you know the one we go to sometimes?'

'What did they do, Lewis?' I whispered.

'They beat me up, they hit me all over my body, and they touched my willy and bum and did the same bad things as Daddy did with his willy.'

This was just too much. This was hell on earth.

'Which of Daddy's friends, sweetheart?' *I had to keep calm.*

'The ones with no wives. Jez. I can't remember the other one's name.'

Jez. Jeremy! And Adam? The gay couple. Adam was visibly uncomfortable in my presence the last time I saw them.

'They started doing it to me before we got the black floor in the kitchen, remember the white floor, Mummy?'

I nodded and stroked his hair. *I had been on the hen do in Kraków, and I had returned to find Lewis completely out of it. I thought he was just tired. Damian had said Adam and Jeremy had been over...*

The following morning, I opened Facebook and searched through Madford's timeline until I found a photo of Jeremy and Adam. Showing Lewis my phone, I asked, 'Are these the men Lewis?'

'Yes, Mummy.' His face turned pale. 'Mummy, can I go and play now?'

'Of course, you can, sweetheart.'

They lived next to a primary school and a meadow that was very isolated in parts. Jeremy was charming and intellectual. Adam was witty and friendly. They were hedonists, like Madford. The rent boys…the drugs…

That evening, I knew what was coming. Once again, we lay in the dark and once again Lewis started to open up.

'Grandad Bill said to me at Christmas, "If you tell someone what Daddy's doing, you will never be able to see your Mummy again." Grandma Jean was there and Daddy. Grandma Jean said, "If you tell anyone, all your family will all move to a different home, and you'll never see your family or your pets again." They wrote it on my hand so I wouldn't forget.'

Hospitable, church going, flower-arranging Jean.

'I was opening my Christmas presents, and then Daddy shouted for me to go upstairs. I thought he had another present. He did that horrible thing to me. All the time he was saying, "It isn't real and it's not happening."'

My head was spinning. I had to keep calm.

'Granddad Bill and Grandma Jean are the boss of Daddy. Grandma was badder than Daddy, and Granddad Bill was even badder than Grandma. He did all the same bad things that Daddy did to me.'

'You're safe now, none of them can hurt you anymore,' I told him, stroking his perfect hair, running my fingers down his back. *How could a dad to that to his own child?*

***

Two excruciating weeks had passed since life as I knew it had changed forever. The magic of Christmas was a stark contrast to the daily horrors that Lewis was gradually divulging. Christmas music was constantly playing in the background, and I had a daily delivery of packages from Amazon. The table was full of sequins, tiny bells, string, felt and glue. I had just taught Lewis had to stitch fabric and he proudly showed me his first creation.

'Look, Mummy, I made a little bag for the tooth fairy!' He pressed the handmade bag into my hand.

'Wow, Lewis, that is amazing!' I said, wiping a tear from my eye.

He looked up at me. 'Mummy...' Lewis's tone was different.

I braced myself.

'I thought Daddy was putting poison in me.' He stared down at the needle he had used for sewing his little bag.

'What do you mean, Lewis? What was the poison?'

'It was like a little injection that he put in me. It made me feel sick.'

What did he mean?

Daniel suddenly appeared at the side of me, handing me a LEGO figure he had made. 'Look, Mummy, look!'

That evening I wrapped the rest of the boy's gifts. It was about one in the morning when I finally finished. I looked at the two mountains of presents. There was more than I could afford, or they needed, but I was desperate to compensate Lewis for everything he was going through, and I didn't want little Daniel feeling left out.

'Father Christmas has been Mummy!'

I awoke to yelps of delight from downstairs. They were both sat gleefully tearing their way through their gifts. It was a precious sight. Their little faces filled with joy.

'Wow! Just look at all those presents!' Lewis made a vague attempt to count his, before getting bored and ripping another parcel open. I plonked myself down on the carpet next to them, watching them, until they had finished. Daniel crammed a whole chocolate reindeer into his mouth. Lewis laughed.

It wasn't long before the room was soon one big pile of wrapping paper. I spent the morning inserting batteries and connecting games consoles. As I helped Daniel on with his Power Ranger outfit, he said, 'Last Christmas when we were in Devon, Lewis was crying because Daddy and Grandma and Granddad were breaking his toys.'

Lewis, overhearing from the bathroom, shouted, 'They did do that, Mummy!'

'What a terrible thing to do.'

Why had I ever let him have them over Christmas?

'Come on, boys, we better get ready. Mama Bear, Aunty Nonie and James will be here shortly,' I said.

When everyone had had their fill of Christmas dinner, we relaxed in the lounge. Daniel was sat quietly playing with his Octonauts when he suddenly spoke, 'Daddy put his willy in my mouth, and he wee'd in my mouth.' He paused, as he pressed one of the Octonauts into their matching boat. 'Daddy said, "How much do you want to drink some wee wee? Drink this magic wee wee, it's really good for you."' He pushed his little boat around on the carpet for a few seconds. 'Then he put my pull-up on, and wee wee just comes out of my bum.' He looked up at me. 'I concentrate not to wee, but it just comes out.'

The room fell completely silent, aside from the sound of the games console that Lewis was playing on. Mum got up from her chair and knelt on the carpet next to Daniel. 'I'm so sorry that happened to you,' she spoke softly. 'Sweetheart, I promise you nothing like that is ever going to happen to you ever, ever again.'

She looked up at me, her face contorted.

I couldn't speak. *Not Daniel, too! Please God, don't say he'd done this to both my boys.*

Tears streamed down my face as I ran from the lounge.

'I didn't mean to make Mummy sad,' my beautiful child told my mum.

'You didn't, Daniel, I promise you, it wasn't you,' I

heard Mum's reply.

The following day, Boxing Day, Lewis woke up with a start.

'I had a bad dream Mummy, about Daddy and his band,' he explained when I came rushing through from my room.

'There, there, it's okay, Lewis.' I reached out my hands and encased his in mine. 'It's just a bad dream. How about I go and make you some delicious pancakes, with lots of Nutella?'

'Yes, please.'

'We'll come over to yours again today, love,' Mum said on the phone.

'Okay. Good.'

The thought of leaving the house, our safe place, had now become a scary thought.

'The boys will want to play with their new toys,' she added.

After lunch, we decided to watch some telly. David Attenborough was on, much to Lewis's delight. He sat intently in front of the tv. Daniel was showing Naomi his Power Rangers. 'Look, Aunty Nonie. Look at these cool guys.'

'Cool. What's this one called?' She asked, picking up a red Power Ranger.

'He's called "Red".'

Daniel took the toy off Naomi. Suddenly, he began to bang the toy hard on the sofa. He paused, looking up at his aunty with glistening eyes. 'By the way, Daddy's a bad man cos he does scary things to us.'

'What scary things does he do, Daniel?' Naomi asked.

'Daddy killed me. I was just dying. He put me in the bath and kept holding me down. He killed me.'

Grabbing my notepad, I scribbled down more words.

This was my life now, bearing witness in scant shorthand to the horrific abuse my son's kept disclosing, abuse suffered at the hands of their father.

***

One day blended into the next into the next. Between the chaos of Christmas and the devastation of Damian, time had lost all meaning. There was a stillness in the air that morning. The boys were unusually quiet. The cats lay fast asleep curled up on the windowsill. The fairy lights looked dimmer than usual. Outside a low mist hung over the still trees, that stood there bare, as if in mourning. Pulling up a chair, I sat down at the dining table where Daniel was colouring. He looked up from his drawing pad and placed his felt tip down.

'Daddy kills babies.'

I looked at him. *I must have misheard.*

'He just got the magic wand, and the baby was dead. Then he put its nappy back on.' Daniel looked over at Lewis, who was sat with his hands clasped over his ears in the adjoining lounge. He continued with his drawing. I looked over at the paper.

'That's Daddy.' He pointed to the central figure on the page. A menacing black figure holding a stick. I studied his drawing. 'That's the baby.' He moved his finger and pointed to a tiny circle with sticks as arms and legs, lying on the table. 'That's the blood,' he continued. The red scribble took up most of the baby's body and spilled onto the floor below. 'Those are all the other guys.' He pointed to all the other figures that were standing around the table with the baby on it.

'Who were the other guys, Daniel?'

'I don't know. They had cloaks on and masks.'

Lewis got up from the sofa walked over and sat next to me. 'One of them was Grandma Jean. I could tell because her shoes were sticking out from under the cloak.' His voice was barely a whisper.

'There's loads of them,' Daniel explained.

"Where's the dead baby?" Wasn't that what Lewis had asked, when he woke up terrified, months ago?

Five

It was New Year's Eve. The boys were huddled together on the carpet in front of the television watching *Octonauts* on TV, leftover pancake crumbs on plates pushed to the side. As I looked outside onto the quiet cul-de-sac and the hills, it dawned on me that it had now been over three weeks since DI Karen Wright had said that she would be assigning another officer to the case, after my complaint about DC Webster. *Time was ticking. The boys would need to be examined.* Finishing the last mouthful of my toast, I waited until the TV show had finished.

'Boys, we need to get ready to go to the doctors. Then we can bake fairy cakes.'

'No!' Daniel screamed, throwing himself backwards onto the carpet.

'What is it, sweetheart?' I scooped up my hysterical child, sitting him on my lap.

'D-Daddy will be there,' he sobbed.

'No, sweetheart, he won't be there.' I wiped away a tear that was running down his cheek and hugged him close.

Lewis turned around. 'Mummy, I know why Daniel is

saying that. It's because Daddy pretends to be a doctor and then does horrible things to us.'

I gasped and quickly masked the horror that must have been drawn across my face.

'Last time he did that, I got away, but he caught Daniel, and then he injected him.'

My mind flashed back to the last time I saw Damian. He stood at the front door whilst Daniel stood crying unconsolably in the hallway. I was bundling him up in his coat, hugging him, telling him he would be okay and that Daddy loved him. Then I packed him and Lewis off with him. I shuddered.

'Boys, nothing bad is ever going to happen to you again. I promise.' I pulled them both close in a group hug.

Dr West was a woman. I had specifically asked for a female doctor. Hearing my name being called, we walked through the reception, to her door. I knocked.

'Come in,' a matronly like voice called.

As we walked through into the bright room we were greeted with a smiley face, looking across from the other side of the desk.

'Hi, boys.'

'Hi,' the boys replied, as they climbed onto two of the chairs to the side of the room.

'So, how can I help you today, Amanda?' the doctor asked kindly.

'My sons have disclosed sexual abuse by their father and others,' I blurted out.

Dr West immediately sat forward in her chair.

'We haven't been offered sexual health checks and it's been almost a month since they last saw him,' I explained.

'I am so sorry. But I can't carry out those checks here. The police should have organized them for you.' She sighed frustrated as she started tapping at her computer keyboard. 'I'm going to call social services. You should expect a visit from them later.'

That evening, we sat expectantly in the Christmassy lounge of our new house, fairy lights twinkling on the tree that was starting to wilt. The aroma of cake and buttercream filled the air. It was New Years' Eve for the rest of the world, and their celebrations were just beginning whilst we sat quietly waiting for social services. James twiddled his thumbs, Naomi had that permanent look of worry that was becoming a feature, and dear Mum kept pacing the room, sighing. At last we heard a knock at the door. I jumped to my feet.

'Hi, Mandy, this is DC Alice Scott,' Keith Dawson, the social worker, said after I opened the door.

DC Scott, a young woman in police uniform, smiled at me. Her dark hair hung either side of her pretty face.

'Good to meet you. Please come in.' I hoped I didn't sound as anxious as I felt. 'Can I get you both a drink?'

'No, thanks,' Mr Dawson replied.

DC Scott shook her head.

'This is my mum, Dianne. And this is my sister, Naomi, and her partner, James.' I said, as I took them through to the living room.

'We'll go upstairs and play board games with the boys,' Naomi said to James.

Keith took out his notebook as DC Scott began the conversation. 'So, Amanda, your GP contacted us earlier to say you had requested sexual health checks for the boys?'

'Yes, the boys have now made more disclosures. Rape, injections, other abusers…' I said, aware that my voice and hands were trembling.

DC Scott pulled out a pocketbook and started making notes. Mr Dawson was already filling his pad with an eloquent scrawl. 'Okay, so I'd like you to go through the boy's disclosures first, Mandy. Then I'd like to talk to Lewis.'

DC Scott continued to write, as I read out the notes from what used to be my red and white spotty dream book. Page after page, I cited the boy's recollections in the haphazard, sporadic way they told me. Closing the book and placing it on my lap, I looked from one of them to the other. Neither returned my stare. Instead, they continued to write. The sound of two consecutive pens moving across paper lasting for several minutes.

'Okay, I'll book in sexual health checks for next week. Although, after all this time, it's likely that any trauma and tearing to the skin would have healed by now. They should have been offered a check straight after Lewis's first interview,' DC Scott spoke in a calm and measured way.

'What about the injections that Lewis described?' I asked.

'We can ask the doctor to also take hair samples from the boys to be tested for drugs,' she replied. 'I'll book them in for the day after tomorrow when the clinic opens again. Can you go and get Lewis now?' she added.

I left the room and went upstairs. There was laughter coming from the bedroom. I walked into the large pale blue and white room crammed full of new toys. Lewis and Daniel were sitting in the middle of the floor with Naomi and James, playing "Buckaroo". Little Daniel squealed with delight as he placed a bucket on the donkey's saddle.

'Lewis, sorry to spoil your game, could you come and meet Alice the police-woman?'

'Okay, Mummy.' Lewis climbed to his feet. His face changed from happy to concerned.

'She's nice,' I whispered to him as we walked hand in hand downstairs. 'Lewis, this is Alice.'

'Hi, Lewis, it's lovely to meet you. Wow, you're tall for

a seven-year old.' DC Scott outstretched her hand to shake his. Lewis smiled and took her hand.

'Hi, Lewis,' Mr Dawson echoed his colleague. He had been sitting quietly taking notes. 'I'm going to write some stuff down, whilst you talk to Alice.' He smiled.

'Okay.' Lewis looked nervous.

'So, tell me what you've been playing upstairs?' Alice asked playfully.

'Buckaroo. Have you ever played it?' Lewis's face loosened a little.

'I have indeed,' Alice replied. 'We'll have to have a game one day?'

Lewis nodded.

Alice's face took on a more serious look. 'Okay, it's a deal! But, tonight I'm here to find out about everything you have been telling Mummy. Do you think you could tell it again to me?'

'Okay. But can you ask them to go out of the room?' he whispered loudly to her.

Alice looked over at me and Mum.

'Come on, Mandy, let's go up and see the others.' Mum tugged at my hand gently.

I didn't want to leave my son alone, but I didn't want to stay if he didn't want me to.

***

'What's going on here then, Daniel?' I asked as I sat down next to my youngest upstairs.

'A pirate game, Mummy. I'm winning Aunty Nonie and James.' he giggled. 'Do you want to play?'

'Sure do!' I lied.

We must have played ten games, maybe more.

'Mummy, try harder!' Daniel scolded.

At last, the bedroom door suddenly swung open.

'Right, Mummy, you can go downstairs now.' Lewis

said, sitting down next to James. 'What are you playing? I want a go.'

'Okay, sweetheart.' I stroked his flushed red cheek.

'Well done, love,' Mum whispered to him as we left the room.

'Well, he said a lot.' DC Scott looked down at her notepad as Mum and I returned tentatively to the lounge. Keith Dawson looked up, nodding in agreement.

'Lewis described Daddy putting his willy in his bum. He told me that Jez and the other man hit him and touched him all over his body. He said, "There was no stopping them." He told me about the injections, and he told me that Grandma Jean and Granddad Bill did bad things to him too.'

Alice paused. 'I think he wanted to protect you both, and that's why he asked to speak to me alone.'

My eyes started to fill up. I looked away. Mum was pacing the room. Alice stood up whilst Keith zipped up his bag.

'I'm going to have Jeremy and his friend arrested. We will ask Mr Madford to come in and be questioned again, and I'm going to send someone down to Devon to the grandparents.'

'What about the boys?' Mum asked, her face creased with worry.

'Well, I definitely need to interview Lewis again. Daniel can have a play interview as he's under five. But first, I would like to meet the boys a couple of more times, to build a rapport with them.' Alice sounded both matter of fact and warm when she spoke.

***

After a forty-minute car journey we arrived at the modern looking building. The large NHS sign read, Sexual Assault Referral Centre. The receptionist was bright and bubbly, as if she hadn't figured out where she was working. She led us down a corridor and into a room with brightly coloured shiny plastic chairs and bright white walls.

The boys immediately made a bee-line for the large lava lamp in the corner, momentarily transfixed with the bright purple blobs slowly changing shape and reforming.

'Mama Bear, look at this!' Daniel shouted gleefully.

'Dr Sullivan will be with you in a minute,' the receptionist said with that same sense of brightness, like she was auditioning for the Disney Channel.

Dr Sullivan was a quiet lady with mousy hair. She appeared after a few minutes, clutching a file and looking down slightly. 'Hi, I'm here to see Lewis and Daniel,' she said. 'but first of all, can I speak to Mum?' She squinted up at me.

Dr Sullivan lead me into a small room at the other end of the corridor. The sun streamed into the bright room, making it too warm. 'Please, take a seat. I'm just going to ask you a few questions, if that's okay?'

'Yes, that's fine.'

'Right then, can you start with Lewis' first disclosures and go from there?'

I blurted out everything I had heard over the past month until Dr Sullivan interjected.

'Injections, you say?' She looked up, screwing up her nose.

'Yes, that's what Lewis told me. Can you take hair samples from the boys?'

She paused. 'I don't think there would be any need to do that.'

'What?' *Why would she say that?* 'It all makes sense now, Lewis's extreme behavioural, emotional and educational problems over the years.' I was conscious that I was speaking fast, but I wanted her to know how long it had all been going on, how much the boys had been through.

'He could be on the autistic spectrum,' she replied, smiling slightly.

'My son's problems were caused by the abuse.' I gulped, as I tugged at the sleeves of my cardigan.

'Okay, well I need to have a chat with Lewis and Daniel, and after that I'll examine them. Can you go and get Lewis please?'

Holding Lewis's clammy hand, the doctor inspected first the upper part of his body, and then from the waist down. His cheeks flushed. I squeezed his hand and smiled at my brave boy.

'I can see that Lewis has had molluscum contagiosum? The scars are on his buttocks and anus.'

'Yes, he had it a couple of years' ago,' I replied. 'Can the disease be sexually transmitted?'

'Yes, it can, but it can also be passed, skin to skin, in children,' she replied. 'Okay, Lewis, you can get dressed now.'

'Thank goodness for that!' he replied, quickly pulling on his clothes.

'Are you going to take the hair samples now?' I asked.

'Well, just give me a minute whilst I find the scissors and a suitable bag.' She scuttled to the other side of the room near the window and searched out the items. 'Okay, Lewis, I need you to sit still whilst I cut a bit of your hair off.' There was the distinct sound of scissors slicing through hair. 'I will be sending this off to the police forensic department for analysis.' She said, carefully sealing the hair into the sample bag.

'It feels really spiky!' Lewis said, running his fingers over the bare patch at the back of his head.

Taking Lewis back into the waiting room where Mum was playing with Daniel, I took my youngest son's hand.

'Sweetheart, it's your turn now. Let's go and see the lady.'

Dr Sullivan smiled as Daniel walked into the room. 'I just need to have a quick look at the rest of your body, Daniel. Mummy is going to help you get ready.'

'No!' Daniel screamed at the top of his voice.

'Sweetheart, the doctor is here to help. She just wants to have a quick look. It won't hurt, I promise.'

'No!' his eyes were filling up with tears.

'Okay, we'll leave it then. Let's just cut a little bit of your hair, Daniel, and then you can go.'

With Dr Sullivan having collected evidence and Alice Scott on the case, I was feeling hopeful. That first DC had been too inexperienced and easily taken in by Damian. This new woman, she'd look after the boys and put their evil father behind bars, where he couldn't hurt any of us ever again.

***

At home I was the strong and protective mother for my sons. A rock for them to start to feel safe and secure. I'd always have a smile on my face and keep the tone light and upbeat but inside I was dying. The realisation of what horrors I had heard coming from the mouths of my babes would hit me at the most unexpected times. Silent screams would tear through my entire body, in the queue at Asda or as I went for a quick run, whilst Mum kept an eye on Lewis and Daniel. Sometimes I would go for a drive alone, so that I could yell at the top of my voice, until my throat felt raw.

It was a couple of weeks after the examination, and Alice came round for her third visit with Lewis and Daniel. As agreed, I left them all together to allow her to develop a connection with the boys. She appeared to naturally like children and both mine had warmed to her.

'Wow! Thank you, boys, for a fantastic time,' she said,

as she scooped up the props, felt tip pens and colouring books.

She came into the kitchen, where I was chopping a bag of carrots for soup. Walking over to me at the sink, she kept her voice low. 'I think it would be a good idea to interview the boys in a couple of days. Lewis is engaging much better now. He's so much easier to work with now he hasn't seen his father for a few weeks.

I nodded, wordlessly, relieved that the investigation was finally moving forward.

***

We were back in the police station. The grey building was as imposing as the last time, with its maze of corridors, where we walked past disused police cells, and into the interviewing rooms.

'Hi, boys!' Alice warmly greeted Lewis and Daniel. 'Would you like a hot chocolate?'

'Yes, please,' both boys said at once.

'Daniel, I'm going to speak to you first, okay, in this room over here?'

Daniel nodded. He toddled off behind Alice, wrapped up in his warm hand knitted cardigan. He looked like a baby.

'Bye, sweety,' I tried to keep my voice upbeat as I watched my tiny three-year-old son head off with the Detective Constable. Time ticked on in the small waiting room, Lewis was starting to get restless. He scrambled through boxes of grubby plastic toys that were only suitable for toddlers, and books that he couldn't read.

'Mummy, this is rubbish. I hate it in here!' he grumbled.

'I know, love.' My heart went out to him.

'I'm bored waiting for Daniel. When will he be finished?'

'Soon, Lewis, any minute now. How about a game of

"I spy with my little eye"?' I'll start. I spy with my little eye something the colour of red.'

'Handbag?' Lewis suggested.

I shook my head.

'Fire truck!' he squealed, pointing at a sad little engine that was well past its prime.

'Well done!' I enthused.

We somehow managed to keep the game going until Alice appeared with Daniel. 'Okay, Lewis, it's your turn now.'

Lewis gave me an anxious look before scrambling to his feet. 'At last! Then I want to go home,' he told Alice.

Alice led Lewis off into the same room. This would be harder for him; he'd seen more. I hated having to put my sons through this after all they had been through already. Daniel immediately sat on the floor and found a toy. It was a talking phone.

"Daddy! Daddy! Daddy!" the voice on the phone said on repeat.

Mum grimaced as Daniel hit the toy with his fist.

'Shut up, I hate you, Daddy!' he said, his little voice breaking.

'How about this toy, precious?' Mum handed Daniel a power ranger figure. All I could think about was Lewis being quizzed about his horrific abuse for the second time. I twisted the end of my cardigan until it started to fray.

A gruelling hour and a half passed when Lewis finally came through the door and practically collapsed onto my lap.

'There, there, sweetheart.' I said, rocking him gently.

'He did really well, didn't you, Lewis?' Alice said

Lewis looked up. 'I hated it, Mummy,' he whispered to me.

'You brave, brave boy,' Mum said, reaching over to

squeeze his hand.

'Lewis, I just need a quick chat with your mum,' Alice told him.

I gently stood up, and Lewis immediately went to cuddle into Mum's arms. I followed Alice back to the interviewing room. The air was thick with the words that had been spoken in here over the past few hours.

'So, Daniel said that Daddy had wee'd in his mouth.' Alice came straight to the point. 'And Lewis said that Daddy had put his willy in his bum, and that other men Jeremy and Adam had done everything that Daddy had done. But to be honest, I don't think it will be enough evidence for Damian to be charged.'

'Why not? Daniel said how daddy wee'd in his mouth, Lewis described being raped by him, and Jeremy and Adam!' I was conscious my voice was raised, but she was making no sense.

Alice gave me a sympathetic look. 'I believe them,' she said quietly, maintaining eye contact. 'And it will be enough evidence for family court.'

Family court? What had that to do with anything?

'When will we find out the results from the boy's hair samples?' I asked. Surely, that evidence would change things?

'I haven't heard anything about that yet,' Alice replied.

A few weeks more passed, and we still hadn't received the results for the hair analysis. I decided to call DI Karen Wright. 'Hello, Karen Wright speaking.' Her strong Northern Irish accent rang down the phone.

'Hello, it's Amanda Taylor,' I said. 'Have you received the results back yet from the hair samples?

'No.' Her tone seemed abrupt, and I was a little taken back.

'Do you know when they will be back?'

'No, I don't.' She was definitely snapping at me.

'It's just that Lewis disclosed that his father would inject him and Daniel, so I'm keen to get the results,' I continued, my voice faltering.

There was silence at the end of the phone.

'They also both described being abused by lots of men,' I continued.

'Injections? Other men? This sounds fantastical!' she snorted.

'What did you just...I can't believe what I'm hearing...Will you meet me? I think that...'

She interrupted me before I could even finish a sentence. 'No!' she snorted. 'Goodbye.'

I slowly sank down the wall until I was a crumpled heap on the carpet. Burying my head down into my knees, I began to sob.

***

The long harsh winter, with its bitter lies and broken promises laid bare and exposed like the naked trees, gradually turned into spring. Little shoots of green emerged in the garden, followed by bunches of bright yellow daffodils, offering a glimmer of hope as life went on in the strange way that life now was. Bit by bit, I put the boys back together, never mentioning to them the debauched police investigation, and in order to survive, rarely thinking of it myself.

***

It was Easter Sunday, and Lewis and Daniel were tearing into their Easter eggs as the morning sun streamed in through the bright airy lounge.

'Mummy, can you open this?' Daniel passed me a little bag containing sweets.

I carefully opened the packet. 'There you go, sweetheart.'

I handed him back the little bag of brightly coloured sweets. Lewis unwrapped a large chocolate egg. Pausing, he shook his head, and threw the egg on the ground.

'What did you do that for?' I asked him. It wasn't like either of my kids to discard sugar.

'Daddy used to give us sweets after they did bad things to us,' he explained quietly.

Daniel nodded his head in agreement.

'Lewis, who were "they"?' I asked, hoping the panic in my voice didn't show.

'It was the guy who was in Daddy's band. Liam and Alanna's dad,' he said.

'And the other guys from Daddy's band. One of them had a pet snake. Remember? Remember?' Lewis demanded of me.

Grabbing my iPhone, my hands shaking as I scrolled through Facebook, I held the phone in front of Lewis, so he could see the photograph of Damian's band at their last gig.

'Here, sweetheart. Which guys?'

'Him, him and him.' He pointed, without hesitation.

I looked at who he'd picked out. It was the keyboard player, Ken Davey, the percussion player, Gavin Pearce, and the guitar player, Stan Lee.

'That one with the pet snake, he rubbed poo on my face.' He pointed to Stan Lee. His face had turned pale. 'And that one, he punched me hard in the stomach.' He pointed to Gavin Pearce.

I was not sure how I retained my composure but somehow I did. If I showed too much emotion right now, the boys might stop talking.

Daniel sat closer, leaning in to look at the photo. 'Yes, Mummy, he did that to Lewis,' he said, nodding. 'He did that.'

113

Taking a deep breath, I put my iPhone down. 'Boys, this is never going to happen to you ever again,' I promised.

'The other guy was Liam's dad,' Lewis continued.

I picked up the phone again. 'This one? Ken?' I asked.

'Yes, Liam's mum did bad things to us too.' Lewis's demeanour changed, as if he was transported back to his horrific past. I stroked his cheek.

'It's okay, sweetheart.' I wrapped my arm around him as he leaned into me.

'Mummy can we watch *Tinkerbell and the Neverbeast*?' Daniel pleaded, wiping his messy face.

Pulling him close with my other arm, I kissed his chocolate cheek. 'Yes of course, sweetheart.'

I found the disc and placed it into the DVD player and sat in between the boys on the sofa, an arm around each of them, like a mother bird protecting her babies. As the film played, a stream of realisations sped through my mind, like a highspeed train.

***

All Damian's strange behaviour… His obsession with getting me pregnant so soon… the computer that he was so desperate to dump…Damian's father's hold over him …His dad's hold over the whole family … Jean's strange comment when Lewis was a newborn…My encounter with Elaina in the play area…Jeremy and Adam's hostility towards me…Damian's band member's acting weird around me …Lewis' stammer…his facial tic…the nightmares and night sweats…the extreme separation anxiety…the boys' screaming about going to their father's…when Lewis said wee had come out of his bottom…the boil on his bottom from being injected…

Lewis' inability to cope with any stress…Lewis' problems at school….the bruises on Lewis' back…the disease on Lewis' bottom and anus…Lewis' depression…Lewis asking where the dead baby was … eating problems with both of my sons…the sexualised behaviour of both Lewis and Daniel…Daniel's anger…the headaches and stomach aches after returning from their father's…the time when I turned up early to collect Daniel and Damian took ages to answer the door …Daniel not responding sitting and staring straight ahead…the odd feeling around Damian and his housemate Mark when they were waiting for me to go…the unexplained cash…the regular trips to Holland and Belgium…

Taking me to family court for overnight stays and holidays…Damian's lack of emotion…his lack of empathy…how he had only wanted me to have his children…why he never talked about his childhood…why he wasn't interested in sex with me …Lewis asking where the dead baby was… Daniel asking why his daddy always showed his willy…the times when Damian would carry the boys straight up to bed after they had spent the day with him…the prolonged bed wetting…Lewis waking up in the middle of the night telling me how much he loved me… Lewis asking where the dead baby was…

***

That evening after the boys had fallen asleep, I decided I had to search Facebook. I had rarely been on at all since this whole nightmare began. I scrolled through the profiles of the three band members. I paused when I saw a photograph of Damian Madford with two other men. I studied the picture. The date was the 11th December 2014. The day after his arrest. It looked like a Christmas do. But Damian was wearing his winter jacket. The other men were wearing dinner jackets. I looked at the names of the other two men. Duncan Lee and Paul Bell. Lee? It dawned on me that he was the brother of Stan Lee. I quickly rang Naomi.

'Have a look at the photo I've just sent you.'

'Yes, that's Duncan Lee on the right,' Naomi rushed her words together. 'He served years in prison for the rape and attempted murder of his ex-wife.'

The following evening both boys were curled on the sofa wating tv. Daniel was starting to get a bit restless, and it was annoying his brother.

'Come up here and draw something,' I told him.

He climbed onto a chair next to me at the dining table. He brought with him his drawing pad and a box of crayons. He took out a black crayon, a red crayon and a brown crayon. Finding a blank page in his drawing book, he quietly started drawing. I looked over at Lewis, who was lost in his programme. Good, I liked it when I could tell his mind was fully occupied. Other than the cartoon background, the room fell quiet for a few minutes, whilst I sipped my tea and ate a piece of leftover chocolate.

Daniel's voice broke the silence. 'Mummy, this is Daddy's office.'

He slid the piece of paper over to me. Bracing myself I inspected his drawing, I sensed Daniel's large brown eyes burning into me.

'Those are all the bad Daddies.' He pointed to a mass of crayoned stick figures, all crowded into what looked like a room. 'That's Daddy.' Daniel pointed to a single stick figure. 'One hundred pounds please.' He spoke in a gruff voice.

'Who says that, Daniel?'

'Daddy, of course.' He looked at me like I was stupid. 'We had to work for Daddy and then loads of men gave Daddy money. Daddy's got lots and lots of money.'

Lewis had remained quiet until now. Then he suddenly spoke as he walked over to the dining table. 'Daddy got lots of men to do bad things to us in the office,' he shouted at me. 'And in other places. In houses. You dropped us off at the office, remember, Mummy?' His big eyes locked onto mine.

I felt like I might vomit. 'Yes, I do remember, sweetheart.' I reached out to touch him, but he flinched.

'Daddy would close the blind in his office. Then he would give me an injection in my bum. He took me into another room and lots of men would be waiting outside, in a line. Jez and that guy were always there. And Mark, the guy who lived with Daddy.'

'Who were the other men, Lewis? Do you know any of their names?'

Lewis shook his head. 'No, sorry, Mummy. Daddy told them not to say their names, to forget them. And most of them had brown bodies and talked funny.'

I pulled my eldest towards my aching heart. 'You've nothing to be sorry for, Lewis, you hear me?' I tucked my hand under his chin and stared into his terrified face. 'You are the bravest boy in the world.'

'And me, Mummy, too?' Daniel declared.

'The two bravest boys in the world.'

Daniel came to join us for a group hug. Clinging to them both, I could taste the salt as tears streamed down my face.

Damian had asked me to drop the boys off to him at the office. He said he was dropping carpet samples off there and would be taking them to the park. I remember the boys getting upset. 'You'll have a nice time with Daddy' I reassured them. Lewis pointed out his father's office to me – 'that's it, up there, Mummy, with the blinds.' I remember the car park being full and being puzzled as it was a Saturday afternoon. A couple of Pakistani men hung around outside their cars.

I could have checked on the boys. I could have stopped

this.

Six

It was a bright, sunny day in the middle of May. The garden was now in full bloom.

I looked out of the large window to see if I could see any new flowers sprouting up and was greeted by the sight of vivid red poppies swaying in the slightest of breezes. For a few seconds I forgot the pain. I reached up and opened a window to let in some fresh air, just as a car pulled up right outside. A slim woman dressed in a summer dress and sandals got out and started walking towards the house.

'Hello, Amanda, I'm Sergeant Katy Spencer.'

'Oh, hello, I was expecting Alice?' My chest tightened as I opened the door to yet another stranger.

'She's been moved to a new department,' she spoke loudly, which seemed odd. She walked past me, with a familiarity that made me uneasy. DS Spencer was in her late forties, at a guess. She had a stern face, framed with strands of long poker straight hair, dyed jet black. It was a contrast to her pale skin and features. I followed her into the lounge.

'So, you called the department to say your sons had

made more disclosures?'

'Yes, that's right, please, take a seat.'

She had already made her herself comfortable on the sofa. The scent of strong perfume filled the air and made me want to gag. 'Okay, Amanda, can you tell me what your sons said?' Her voice had a coldness to it.

Reaching for my red and white spotty notebook, I began to read out the latest horrors. My words came out breathy and rushed, as I felt an air of impatience coming from DS Katy Spencer. My anxiety further heightened when I realised that she wasn't taking notes.

'I have names,' I said, looking up.

'Okay, what are they?' she asked.

It felt like I was annoying her. I listed the band members who had been pointed out, and some of the other friends of Damian's who had been mentioned or described. DS Spencer interrupted when I got to Stan Lee, the guitar player. Taking out her note pad she scribbled something down.

'Stan Lee?' she repeated his name.

'Yes,' I nodded.

This seemed to interest her.

'There's been a conviction of a 'Lee' but it's not Stan, it's Duncan,' she said. 'He was convicted for rape and attempted murder.'

'Yes. Duncan is Stan Lee's brother,' I replied.

I remembered the photo on Facebook of Damian with two other men. One was Duncan Lee, Stan Lee's brother.

'There's something else I need to tell you. Lewis described being abused by several men at his father's office, and I've noticed that there's CCTV next door at the entrance to some flats. Could you check the camera to see if you can get footage?'

'No, we can't do that,' she said, glancing at her watch.

'Why not?'

'I would have to hear it from the boys. And I am not going to request that they are interviewed again.'

'So, what are you going to do about these disclosures?' I asked, my voice barely a whisper. *Nothing. Nothing will be done.*

'I'll pass it onto the CPS and add it to your existing file,' she said, getting up to leave.

I couldn't face walking her to the door. Moments later, I heard the sound of loud music blaring from her car. I looked out of the window and saw her applying lipstick in the rear-view mirror before speeding off. My eyes fell on to the blooming poppies. Why weren't the police investigating? Why were they not testing the boy's hair samples for drugs? Was this all because I had complained about DC Webster? How could we stay here if the police weren't taking us seriously? Every question led to same answer, if the police weren't going to charge Madford then we couldn't stay.

***

Within a matter of months, we had abandoned our house and relocated to a small historical market town nestled in between Nottingham and Lincoln. James had already been living there for a couple of years, and we had visited many times, so it made sense. Naomi moved into the enormous, ultra-modern detached house James was renting over-looking the largest park in the town. Me and the boys rented a tiny but quaint "two up, two down" on a leafy road five minutes away. Mum had also rented a small house, close by. I had one bedroom; the boys had the other. Our furniture just about squeezed in, with the exception of a few items that I had to sell on eBay. The loft had been converted and made a fantastic play area, much to the boys' delight. We had a tiny bit of green that passed for a garden.

At least the boys had somewhere outdoors to go. On the upside, there were children of a similar age living next door.

On the first morning in our new home, I awoke to the sun streaming in through the paper-thin curtains. Stretching, I welcomed the new day. It was so much warmer down here. I pulled on some shorts and a t-shirt and opened the window to let in some air before heading downstairs. For the first time in ages I was feeling positive and safe.

'Good morning, little guys!' I smiled at my precious boys who were already up and about and playing in the lounge.

'We like it here, Mummy!' Daniel said, beaming.

'Yeah! It's cool,' Lewis agreed. 'It's like being on holiday.'

The boy's eyes sparkled in a way that I hadn't seen since they were babies.

It was a good move all around, and within a matter of weeks, we had connected with a group of home schoolers and enrolled Daniel at a local school. The boys had made firm friends with the neighbour's children who were in and out of our house every day. Now that they hadn't seen their father in ages, Lewis and Daniel began to blossom in ways I could never have imagined. It was a pure joy to see them happy and relaxed. Lewis had even begun to learn how to read. My heart sang. My children were finally starting to enjoy life.

It was a warm September afternoon when I got a phone call from Sergeant Katy Spencer. I was sitting sipping an afternoon cuppa and flicking through the local paper.

'I'm just ringing to inform you that the CPS have said that there is not enough evidence to proceed,' she said.

'I see,' I replied, sighing. 'What now?'

'That's it I'm afraid. Damian Madford, Jeremy Green and Adam Wood have now been released from their bail terms.'

I looked out of the kitchen window, at the boys playing outside on the decking. They were safe, at least. I could keep them safe. We would just need to be careful that no one found out where we were living. Pushing down the slightly sick feeling at the pit of my stomach, I headed into the garden and picked up the ball that had rolled my way.

'How about a game of piggy in the middle, boys?'

***

Autumn arrived, and with it bursts of vivid red, burnt orange and ochre danced in the tress, before a few nights of storms shook everything to the ground, leaving behind bare branches. The holiday feeling of being somewhere new and warm was also fading. The postman had left a large brown envelope on the floor below the post-box. Picking it up I inspected the stamp in the corner, just about making out the words 'Nottingham Family Court' around the inked crown. Tearing open the envelope, my heart racing as I read the letter. It was an application from Damian Madford. He was asking for shared custody of the boys. I quickly scanned the pages. ***The mother has caused emotional harm to the children by falsely accusing their father of sexually abusing them.'***

The weekend passed in a daze. I focused on the boys and the house, trying to keep myself busy changing sheets and washing the carpet. Every time I thought of the letter, I felt weak with fear and reached for another surface to clean. *No court would let a man accused of gang raping the boys near them. Surely?* But the police had let them all walk free, and I could never have seen that happening.

First thing Monday I rang my old solicitor, Amy Martin, who had represented me a few years back, when

Damian had taken me to court for overnight stays. 'He's got some nerve applying for custody,' she said. 'I don't want you to worry, Mandy. The boys will be assigned a guardian to put forward their views.'

Amy's words rang in my head long after our phone call had ended. It was all well and good for her to say not to worry, but I'd heard that line a few times. At the back of my mind there was a voice urging me to up and leave. To get out of this country and start a fresh in some far-flung place at the other end of the Earth. I could put the house on the market and use the proceeds to set up a new life. But thoughts fleeing quickly left my mind and instead I took the more realistic approach, to accept and face the reality of going through the justice system that was here to uphold the law and protect the vulnerable. The thought of seeing Madford again made my stomach turn.

Shortly after I had instructed Amy, she emailed to inform me that the first hearing had been scheduled. It was to take place at Nottingham Family Court on the 1st December 2015.

I rang Naomi.

'I've got a court hearing on the 1st December,' I blurted out, as she answered the phone in her usual cheery voice.

'Mandy, it'll be fine,' she reassured me. 'James will go to court with you.'

James parked in a large multi-story car park opposite the court. The freezing cold air hit me as I stepped out into it. Shivering, I pulled the collar of my coat up to cover my neck and put on my gloves.

'We're early, let's go for a coffee,' James suggested.

'I'll get the coffees; you go and sit down.'

James joined the queue as I headed over to the seating area. Walking through to the back of the café, I immediately saw the familiar shape of the back of a dark, narrow-shouldered man wearing a pin striped suit, sitting in the corner, facing the wall, reading a newspaper. His black hair slicked down with too much gel. I rushed back to James who was in the middle of ordering the coffee.

'Madford is here,' I whispered. 'Please, can we just go?'

The court was grey and oppressive. Walking through the security area I noticed a woman crying as she left the building. A man in a suit hovered awkwardly at her side. Barristers donning wigs and court ushers carrying clipboards milled around. A blonde-haired, heavily made-up, middle-aged woman suddenly appeared from nowhere.

'Amanda?' she asked, holding out her hand to shake mine.

'Yes. You must be Michelle.'

'Well, I've got us a meeting room. Let's go and talk.'

I got up and followed her. James waited behind. After Michelle had briefed me through the court process, an usher popped her head around the door. 'You're in now,' she said.

I followed my barrister into the court room. It was a little smaller than I had imagined, with three benches laid out facing a raised area for the judge. Madford was already there with a young male barrister. He had dark hair and glasses and a haughtiness about him that mirrored Madford's.

After a couple of minutes of relative silence, the usher spoke. 'All rise.'

Everyone stood up, as the judge, a sixty-something-year-old man, walked in and sat down in the raised chair behind the desk, facing the rest of the room. He smiled and everyone sat down, apart from Damian's barrister who remained standing.

'Your Honour, I am Sebastian Ramsbottom, counsel for the father. This is the case of Madford and Taylor in relation to Lewis Madford, aged eight, and Daniel Madford, aged four. The applicant father is applying for shared custody. The father's position is that the mother has caused emotional harm by leading the two boys into believing that they have been sexually abused by their father. It is unfortunate that Mr Madford hasn't seen his sons since December 2014.'

'Thank you,' said the judge, as he nodded towards my barrister.

'Your Honour, I represent the respondent mother.'

The judge nodded.

'The mother's position is that the boys have indeed been subject to sexual abuse by their father, so therefore she is not in support of any contact with between her sons and the father.' Michelle sounded almost apologetic.

'Thank you,' said the judge.

Sebastian Ramsbottom rose again. 'Your Honour, given the complex and serious nature of this case, I am requesting transfer to a circuit judge.'

The judge glanced over at Michelle. She quickly rose.

'Agreed, Your Honour.'

The judge nodded. 'Permission granted.'

A subsequent hearing was scheduled for the following April in 2016. Four months away. Good. We would have a bit of breathing space.

***

With the first court case behind us and Christmas upon us, we decided to celebrate in style. For a week or so we managed to put the spectre of the looming court case to the back of our minds and concentrate on festivities and making it as special as possible for the boys. Naomi and James's house was the perfect place to host a family Christmas. It sparkled with fairy lights in every room and two of the finest Norwegian Christmas trees on sale locally, one in the kitchen and one in the vast lounge, decorated with beautiful ornaments. The smell of fresh pine and roasted turkey filled the air. Champagne and laughter flowed.

There was an excitement to the atmosphere which was alive with expectation and hope. The boys were healing. Life was good. Justice would come. The family court would protect my sons and keep their father away from them. Once the court case was out of the way, then we could get on with the rest of our lives.

***

It was a cold March morning and I had not long returned home from the school run. Lewis was quietly colouring in as I flicked through the news section on my iPhone. An article caught my eye. "IICSA and Operation Hydrant investigating institutional failure within historical cases of CSA."

I immediately called Mum. 'Can you call them, Mum? Our case *is* classed as historical'

'Yes, I'll call them as soon as I come off the phone,' Mum promised.

'I'm taking Lewis to forest school today. Shall we all come over for tea?'

The few hours in the forest went quickly, with Lewis enjoying activities with his friends and plenty of fresh air. After collecting Daniel from school, I pulled up outside Mum's, so the boys could race over to the back of her house. I watched them running over to hug her as I parked the car.

After the boys had finished their fish and chips followed by ice cream, they settled in front of a film. Mum and I quietly slipped into the small conservatory.

'I was on the phone to the IICSA for four whole hours!' Mum exclaimed as soon as we sat down. 'They're going to put us in touch with a police officer from Greater Manchester Police. They assured me it wouldn't be Wright or Webster.'

'Thank God,' I whispered, barely aware of the tears flowing down my face.

Mum raised her glass of red wine. 'This could be our breakthrough, love.'

A few days' later, my phone rang. *'No Caller ID'*. I quickly answered.

'Hello?'

'Hi, is that Amanda?' A man with a deep voice spoke.

'It is,' I replied.

'Hi, Amanda, my name is Detective Chief Inspector Martin Murray, on behalf of Operation Hydrant. I am going to be looking into the investigation of your case.'

'Oh, great, good to speak to you.'

'Okay, so firstly I am going to have the "ABE" interviews of your sons reviewed,' he explained, 'to see if they meet our standards.' He spoke slowly and deliberately. 'And then I'll be looking into why the officers didn't proceed in testing your sons' hair strands.'

'Are the hair samples still in the forensic department?' I asked.

'Yes, they should be. I'll call you back in a couple of weeks when I've got more to tell you.'

I felt a relief and a lightness after I had spoken to DCI Martin Murray. His straightforward and efficient approach gave me a glimmer of hope. *Maybe Mum was right? Maybe this was our turning point?*

That evening I received an email from my solicitor.

Hi Mandy, I have the DVDs of your sons' police interviews here. I know it's short notice, but are you free tomorrow?

It was far from an ideal day to drive the two-hour trip to Manchester. The rain poured relentlessly the entire journey. Once parked up in Manchester city centre, the rain subsided, and I walked the five-minute walk to my solicitor's office, right in the heart of the city. Stepping into the large modern glass office building I headed over to the reception. A young woman smiled from behind the desk. 'Can I help you?' she asked.

'Yes, I'm here to see Amy Martin,' I told her, adding, 'I'm Amanda Taylor.'

'Okay, can you take a seat and I'll let her know you're here.'

Walking over to a large sofa I took a seat. My stomach began to churn, and I felt faint at the thought of watching my precious sons give their testimonies to the police. Lifting up my head, I could see Amy walking towards me.

'Mandy, how are you?' she said.

'I'm dreading seeing the videos, to be honest,' I confided

'I'm sure you are. Let's go to one of the meeting rooms and get a coffee.'

Amy led me into a bright meeting room, with a large table in the centre. I took a seat opposite the large TV at one end.

'I'll go and get you a coffee, Mandy, you get comfortable. You can take notes, if you wish,' she said. Moments later, Amy reappeared, placing a mug down onto the table.

I wrapped my hands around the mug of hot coffee.

Amy took a seat opposite me and pressed 'play' on the remote control. The DVD started playing. It was Lewis's first ABE interview. I braced myself as I stared at the TV screen in front of me. Then I saw the interviewing room, my boy sat on the sofa. The policewoman sat opposite him on another chair. My precious boy looked so young. Fifteen months had passed, but what a difference? He moved around fidgeting on the sofa.

'Sit still, please, Lewis,' barked the interviewing officer. 'We have even younger children in here than you who manage to behave themselves.'

How could she say that to him? Couldn't she imagine how hard it was to tell a stranger thing he had taken years to tell me? I started to sob.

'Do you want me to pause it, Mandy?' Amy handed me a tissue.

Shaking my head, I continued to watch as the horror in front of me unfolded.

'He made me think that I had done something wrong… He said, "if you tell anyone, then you'll never see Mummy again"'

He repeated "Mummy", and my heart bled.

'What did he do to you, Lewis?'

'He touched me on my willy and on my bum,' he said. 'He always used to lie to Mummy about where he was taking us. He did terrible things to us. He said Granddad Bill did the same things to him when he was little, but "just get over it, it's nothing".' As he said the phrase, his face contorted with anguish. I expected her to pause and try and comfort him, but she seemed to see him more as a suspect than a victim, and certainly not as the frightened child he clearly was. *Where the hell had she got her training?* After just over an hour the interview ended. Amy walked over and put the next disc into the DVD player.

'Do you want to take a break?' she asked, kindly.

I shook my head. I wanted to get out of there. It felt the room was eating oxygen, but I wanted to bear witness to my son's truth.

'This is Lewis's second interview, Mandy. I'm sorry, it must be so difficult for you.'

I controlled my breath by counting silently, and I

controlled my rage by pulling at the threads of my fitted jumper. I watched as my then seven-year-old boy bared his soul to the callous police officer who I'd assumed would take care of him.

'Daddy and Mark went up to the loft. And Jeremy and Adam, sometimes, but this time Daddy and Mark. There was a light coming from the loft. They weren't talking or anything. They were getting the injection stuff out. That's where Daddy kept the injections.'

'How did Daddy do the injection, Lewis?' DC Scott asked.

'Like with a really, really, really, really, really thin needle. So thin that it felt like a mosquito bite.'

'Where was the injection?'

'Here.'

Lewis patted his bottom.

'Whereabouts, Lewis?'

I knew she was a police officer doing her job, but it was devastating to watch my son have to share such detail.

'On my bum cheek.'

'Where did the injection come from, Lewis?' DC Scott didn't miss a beat.

'Daddy. And he got it out of the loft.' Lewis's eyes flashed round the interview room as if he was afraid his daddy might show up.

'What was the injection for?'

'For me. And Daniel. And he said if we ever told anyone then we would never see Mummy again,'

'Did Mark see what Daddy was doing?'

'Of course he did because he was helping him.'

'How was Mark helping him?' the detective asked.

'By doing the same bad things to us as Daddy did.'

'So, what did Daddy do then?'

'Well, he gave me a little injection at first to make me

go to sleep. In fact, it was like this.' Lewis leaned back slowly into the sofa.

'Like that.'

'Using the dolls on the table, Lewis, can you show me where Daddy was when he put his willy in your bum?'

'Like this.'

Lewis positioned the dolls accordingly, and I felt the whole room spin. My precious, precious child, what had they done to him?

'Did Mark do anything to you at this time?'

'No. He did things to Daniel, not me.' Guilt flashed through my son's eyes, as if he'd somehow got off easier.

'You also said to me, Lewis, that your dad's friends, Adam and Jeremy, did things to you as well,' DC Scott's abrasive interviewing style continued.

'Yeah,' Lewis nodded his head as he spoke. He looked so tired, like he'd had enough of the relentless questions.

'What did they do?'

'They put their willy in my bum and hit me.'

Lewis's second interview was finally over. It had taken longer, this one. I got up from my chair, unsteadily.

'I'm going to nip to the loo,' I said, heading out of the meeting room.

Once in the toilet cubicle, I took some deep breaths. All I could think of was getting out of this building and going home to my boys. My beautiful boys. I splashed some cold water on my face and hardly dared look at my haunted eyes, before heading back to the meeting room where Amy was waiting, patiently.

'Okay, Mandy, are you ready for Daniel's interview?' she asked quietly.

I nodded my head and sat down, wringing my hands together as my little boy came into view. He looked and sounded so young. A baby. All wrapped up warm in his knitted cardigan. He sat playing with a soft spider toy and hiding behind the sofa. DC Scott leaned forward on her chair and began talking in a kind of slightly forced sing-song voice.

'Okay, let's play the spider game for a bit then, Daniel, but then I want to ask you some questions.'

'Okay.' Daniel peeped out from around the back of the sofa, his big brown eyes looking fearful.

'Okay, good boy, then after your game, you can start talking about what you told Mummy about what Daddy did?'

Daniel carried on playing with the spider toy. He climbed over the top of the sofa, dropping the toy behind.

'Find it!' he said to D C Scott. She hesitated and then got up from her chair, reckoning to be looking for the toy for a few seconds, until she held it up in the air.

'Here it is!' she sang, although the agitation in her voice was beginning to show. She sat back into her chair opposite Daniel. 'So, Daniel, you're here to see me because you told Mummy about some things about Daddy. Can you tell me exactly what those things were?' Her voice softened a little.

After about half an hour of moving about, my little boy started to open up. 'Daddy's a bad guy. But he was a good guy when Mummy was there. He tells lies, lies, lies, lies.' He started throwing the spider up into the air.

'Daniel, what was it that you told Mummy?'

Give him a chance.

He threw the spider again, but this time DC Scott reached across and took the toy.

'No! Give it back.' Daniel cried, running towards DC Scott, who passed him the toy, shaking her head.

Daniel's little face dropped as he climbed onto the sofa, placing the spider at his side and hugging his knees into his little body. 'He did bad things to us. He made us cry, me and Lewis. We cried and cried and cried.'

'What things does he do, Daniel?' DC Scott asked, her voice softening again.

'He made me drown in the bath.'

'How does he made you drown?'

'He pushed me under the water, and so I can't breathe. He killed me.'

His little cheeks had flushed pink. I wanted to reach inside the screen and pull him away from her, away from it all.

'Me and Lewis are always sleeping when we go to Daddy's. All the time. Sleeping.'

'You were sleeping a lot at Daddy's? Do you know why, Daniel?'

'Of course not. Mummy didn't know either. She didn't know what Daddy was doing to us. But now we're safe. Mummy keeps us safe now.' Daniel stood up. 'I need a wee!' he announced.

DC Scott abruptly got up from her chair. 'Come on then. I'll show you where the toilets are.'

'Then I want to see my mummy.'

My little boy. I bent forward onto the desk and cupped my head in my hands.

'Mandy, not much longer to go now,' Amy said kindly. 'I'll fast forward this bit, for the rest of the interview.'

After a few minutes of Daniel playing with the spider and avoiding DC Scott's questioning, he started to open up again.

'My daddy's a bad guy. He wee'd in my mouth. Daddy's horrible because he's a naughty guy. He doesn't do nice things to us.' Daniel rushed his words together, desperate to be heard.

'What are those not nice things?' DC Scott asked.

'He wees in my mouth and in Lewis's mouth.'

***

It was almost tea-time when I left the solicitor's office, running through the dimly lit streets in the pouring rain. By the time I got back to the carpark I was wet through. Peeling off my saturated coat, I climbed into the car and dried my hands and face with tissues. As I fought to get my breath back, I took out my mobile phone and rang DCI Martin Murray.

'Hello, Martin Murray speaking,' he said in his deep voice.

'Hello, Detective Murray, it's Amanda Taylor. I have just watched the boy's ABE interviews Martin. The boy's hair samples need testing urgently. Lewis gave such clear descriptions.' My words came out rapidly.

'Okay, just answer a couple of questions from me, please, Mandy. When did the boys last see Damian?'

'The 1st December 2014. The day before Lewis's first disclosure.'

'Okay, and when were the hair samples taken?'

'6th January 2015. I can't understand why the police didn't do a test back then?'

'I can't answer that Amanda. I'll instruct forensics to go ahead and analyse the hair samples.'

The drive home seemed to take forever. I fought to concentrate as the rain came down in torrents, and the spray back from lorries flooded my windscreen as I overtook them. Approaching the East Midlands, the downpour eventually subsided. I no longer had to keep my focus on getting safely home. I started to scream. I screamed, and I cried, and I shouted at the top of my lungs. No one could hear me on the windy stretch of road, and I didn't care if they could. My throat felt raw, but my anguish eventually gave way to a sense of calm, and I drove the last part of the journey in silence. Parking the car up outside my house, I could see the front bedroom lit up. Good, the boys were still awake. Walking around to the back of the house, I saw Mum at the window, washing the dishes. She smiled in a knowing way.

'Are you okay, love?' she asked, as I tossed my handbag and soaking coat on the kitchen counter.

'No,' I replied honestly, 'but I have to see the boys right now.' I climbed the stairs to at a time. Daniel was alone in the boy's shared room, tucked into bed, his eyes barely open.

'Hi, Sleepy,' I said, bending down to stroke his soft hair.

'Hi, Mummy, I missed you,' he mumbled.

'I missed you too, darling.' I whispered, leaning in to kiss his cheek before he turned around to face the window, holding onto his favourite teddy. Tiptoeing out, I crept into my bedroom, where Lewis was waiting in my bed. He still slept in my bed, most nights.

'Mummy, where have you been?' Lewis asked.

'I had to go and see a lady in Manchester. I missed you, sweetheart. Come here.' I pulled him close into me, running my fingers through his hair. 'It's late, Lewis, better try and get some sleep.'

'Mummy, can you stay here?'

'Of course, sweetheart,' I promised. 'I'll always be here. Always.'

Seven

Smiling, as I leaned against the doorframe of the back door, I looked out onto the small but perfectly landscaped garden complete with decking, a small patch of grass and raised beds containing bursts of colour. The boys were playing, their laughter filling the air as they threw the ball to one another. They were so happy. The neighbour's dog wagged her tail, desperately wanting to join in with their game as the scent of burning logs wafted over from their firepit. I heard a swishing email alert on my phone. Leaning over the kitchen worktop I clicked onto the correspondence from DCI Murray. *This was it!* The hair analysis report. I opened the first attachment and started reading.

Dear Miss Taylor,

I understand Daniel Madford and his brother Lewis Madford have alleged being sexually assaulted on multiple occasions. This is an historic allegation of sexual abuse against a number of males, one of which is the children's father. It appears that the first allegation was made on the 9th December 2014, which was an initial report of sexual assault. On the 31st December 2014, it has been disclosed that Lewis had been injected in his bum and that, possibly, Daniel had also been injected with an unknown substance. We have been advised by DC Colin Webster that the last contact the children had with their father was August 2014 and that the allegation of the injection of drugs goes back further than this. On the 6th January 2015 a section of hair was obtained from Lewis and Daniel and subsequently submitted for toxicological analysis.

Skimming through the report, my eyes stopped dead at the third page, the table of results.

The hair samples were found to contain the following drugs: Nordiazepam, Temazepam and Zolpidem. These are all sedatives and are commonly used in date-rape…

My head started to spin.

Horrific images of my little boys, lying unconscious on the floor, invaded my mind. Taking a deep breath, I continued to read the report.

…Hair grows at a rate of 1cm per month. For example: if you wish to determine whether the victim had been administered drugs six months ago, then the hair would need to be at least six centimetres long. A period of at least four weeks must pass between the drug being administered and the hair sample being taken.

Pausing for a few seconds, I mentally worked out how the length of time my boys would have been drugged for. Daniel's hair sample measured seven centimetres so that would be around seven months of growth—from around May 2014 to when he last saw Madford on the 1st December 2014. Lewis's hair sample was slightly shorter. I re-read the dates. Something stood out. *We have been advised that the last contact the children had with their father was August 2014. August?* Where had that come from? Had Webster been lying to forensics to protect Madford? Or to 'get back' at me for complaining? Was this why the police had refused to test the boys' hair samples eighteen months earlier? I felt the heat rising in my cheeks as panic spread through my entire body.

'What's up, Mummy?' Lewis appeared at my side, his arm around my back.

'Oh, nothing, sweetheart,' I looked up at his worried little face.

'Tell me, Mummy,' he said, his eyes pleading with mine.

I paused, stroking Lewis's hair, pulling out a stool to sit on. 'Okay, remember when you had your hair samples taken ages ago?'

'Yes.'

'Well the police have finally tested them and there were drugs in your and Daniel's hair.'

Lewis widened his eyes. 'Mummy, I did tell you that Daddy injected me to make me sleepy. Did you not believe me?'

I reached out and took his soft hand into mine. 'Of course, I did, sweetheart.'

'Did the police not believe me?' he asked.

'Yes, it's just taken them a while to test the hair,' I lied.

Lewis's expression suddenly changed, the colour visibly draining from his cheeks. 'Mummy, you know when we had to go to Devon with Daddy?'

'Yes, love.'

'Well, Grandma Jean she gave us sweets. They were wrapped up in 'Haribo' wrappers, two in a pack. But they tasted horrible.'

'Where they Haribo sweets?'

'Definitely not! They were disgusting. Me and Daniel would always be sleeping when we went to Devon.'

I held my breath as Lewis continued.

'And do you know Mummy, Grandma Jean had a special black tin where she kept the sweets and the injection stuff. It had material on the top.'

I shook my head slowly. How could a grandma do this to her own flesh and blood?

139

'I wanted to tell you, Mummy, but I was scared, so I only had Daddy to tell. He used to tell me that I was getting confused, and then we'd play with a swingy thingy, and my eyes would get tired.'

'A swingy thingy?'

Lewis mimed a pendulum.

'Oh, Lewis…Lewis…' my heart hurt.

'Grandma Jean would call you horrible words, Mummy, and said that she would kill you if I told anyone.'

I reached over to Lewis and pulled him onto my lap, encasing him in my arms. It was pure agony to hear what that evil family did to my boys, hugging him close I reassured myself that Lewis was finally starting to feel safe.

***

It was the day of the next court hearing, a humid early summer's day. James had agreed to accompany me again. We parked the car and walked the five minutes down to the now familiar sight of the grey and oppressive building that housed the family court. The cleaners must have just finished as the smell of disinfectant hit me the moment we walked through the automatic doors. Once inside the building I immediately saw Damian Madford in the foyer. My whole body stiffened, and I felt my airwaves constrict as I caught his eye. He looked away quickly and made his way out the door towards the lift.

'Morning.' Michelle, my barrister, appeared at my side.

I jumped. 'Hi,' I replied, quietly.

The three of us went through security and waited for the lift Madford had taken to come back down.

'I'll be over there, Mandy,' James said, giving me a reassuring look, as he headed over to the crowded waiting area.

'I think that meeting room is free,' Michelle said, leading me to a small stuffy room.

We sat down on opposite sides of the table. Michelle took out her file as I took off my suit jacket and pulled my hair back off my forehead.

'Michelle, I take it this hair analysis will be enough to stop Madford from getting access to the boys?' I asked, getting straight to the point.

'Doesn't quite work like that, Mandy. It's compelling evidence, and the judge will certainly take it into account, but there's a process that we have to follow. And the judge will look at all the evidence both sides present, and the case as a whole.'

'Case as a whole, what does that even mean? He's been raping my babies for years, that's the case as a whole.'

Michelle nodded sympathetically. 'Look, Mandy, you just stay calm, try not to react to anything you hear and leave the rest to me. That's why you hired me.'

I didn't reply. She was right, of course. I had to let her do her job and let the system to its job. No judge in his right mind was going to give children to a suspected member of a paedophile ring. As long as I stayed calm and told the truth everything would work out.

Half an hour had passed, and then a court usher knocked on the door. 'You're in now,' she told us.

'All rise.' The cloaked usher loudly announced the judge's entrance. We all stood up as the steely-faced judge glided in.

'Yes?' He smiled at Madford's barrister, Sebastian Ramsbottom, who immediately sprang to his feet.

Ramsbottom was just about old enough to be a barrister. He had that equestrian look found almost exclusively in upper class circles and spoke like someone who had started elocution lessons before he'd learned how to walk.

'Your Honour, this is the case of Madford and Taylor,

concerning the children Lewis and Daniel Madford. It is unfortunate, Your Honour, that counsel for the mother has just, without warning, applied for what the mother describes as "new evidence" in the form of results of a hair strand analysis authorized by Detective Chief Inspector Murray.'

'Yes?' The judge nodded towards Michelle.

She rose to her feet. 'Your Honour, yes, the hair analysis indicates the presence of a number of sedatives that were found in both boy's hair samples that were taken in January 2015.'

The judge peered from behind his glasses. 'What were the drugs?'

'Your Honour, if I may just take a look?'

The judge nodded, and Michelle bent down to her desk for a few seconds and scrutinized the report in her file. 'Your Honour, the hair samples were found to contain nordiazepam, temapazan and zolpidem.'

'What quantities were found?' he asked.

'Low quantities, Your Honour' she replied.

The judge glanced over at me and gave me a stern look. I could feel the colour rising in my cheeks.

Sebastian Ramsbottom stood up and cleared his throat before addressing the judge. 'Your Honour, the father adamantly denies any knowledge of this drugging.'

'Very well,' the judge said, maintaining his eye contact with me. 'This is obviously a complex case with some very serious allegations and counter allegations. I think it's time to bring in some outside experts…

As his voice droned on, I was stuck at the words, "Counter Allegations". What did that even mean? I'd accused him of initiating the gang rape of our children, multiple times. What was he going to accuse me of? Arriving early a few times? Mostly because the boys would beg me to. Calling too often to check in on them? Again, usually at Lewis's request. There things weren't comparable and yet something about how the judge had looked at me had unnerved me. Maybe that's what he did with everyone, so that he appeared impartial.

'Don't worry.' Michelle whispered to me as we left the room.

***

I got home to a house so quiet I could have heard a pin drop. With the boys having a sleepover at Naomi's, I would be on my own, which I was glad about and sad about. The doorbell rang, breaking the silence. Looking out of the bedroom window I saw the postman holding a large packet. I rushed downstairs.

'Afternoon, love.' The postman handed me the package.

I scrawled my name over his delivery pad, gave him a thank you nod and, taking the parcel from him, shut the door quickly. It was from my solicitors, but Michelle hadn't told me to expect it. The trepidation that proceeded every legal document meant my hands shook as I opened the box to reveal a large file. The attached note read, "Police disclosure".

Pulling a stool out from underneath the counter, I sat down. I knew what I was looking for and began leafing through the pages until I came to the section about the hair analysis. Reading the list of email correspondence, I noticed an email between DCI Mick Murray and DC Colin Webster.

Boss, copies of the hair report for your information. Don't think this changes a great deal,
though I think she'll make a great deal of the result. Webster had written.

Webster was still involved. How could this be? I bit the

edges of my finger-nails and continued to flick through the pages. There were minutes of a meeting with social services and other professionals, including Webster. I searched for his name in the text. When asked for his view on Madford's culpability he was quoted as saying, "I believe that the father is innocent."

Pushing the stool back, I started pacing the small kitchen, images of Webster dancing in my head. Him standing in a different kitchen trying to justify why no charges were being brought against Madford. What had he said?

"Fathers have rights…" "Children say these things when their parents break up…" "He's an impeccable character that would stand up well in court…" "You remind me of my ex-wife…" "He doesn't look like a paedophile…"

My head was pounding. I needed fresh air. Abandoning the stack of paper, I headed out to garden. Sitting down on the decking, with the hot sun on my face, and fresh tears of rage and fear falling, it dawned on me that if that if DC Webster had done his job, a warrant would have authorized for a full house search, that would have revealed the date rape drugs, the needles, and God knows what else, and Madford would now be behind bars.

"…he doesn't look like a paedophile." What a dumb thing to say! Does he think I'd have married him if he looked like a paedophile?'

***

As the year progressed, the seasons seemed to end almost as soon as they had begun. I longed for time to stand still, to enjoy each precious moment, but it rolled on with the chaos of child rearing and household management and the court case. At the back of my mind, all the time, the court case…

The date had been set for the fact finding. It was to be

held in February 2017 over ten days. It was still five months away but if the last few months were anything to go by, it would be just around the corner. With each turn of the page on my calendar, I became more anxious.

September marked the start of a new school year for Daniel. He was moving up to Year One. I was so proud of his progress, and secretly amazed. My sweet and kind little Daniel. And Lewis was looking forward to the home-schooling classes starting again. His true nature was blossoming, it made me feel warm inside when I saw him laughing and chatting with his friends.

As I washed the dishes that evening a feeling of dread suddenly took over. *What if this court case was going to implode like the police investigation?* I never saw that coming. All it took was one bad apple. Look at the damage Webster had done. *What if the judge had an ex-wife he hated or kids that hated him, and an ex-wife he blamed for it?* My breath grew shallower as my thoughts spiralled. I focus on slowing it down and felt a sense of calm returning. Webster was my one bad apple. The judge was going to see the hair samples, and he was going to hear the boy's testimonies. *There was no way he'd let either of them near Madford after that.*

***

'Let's all go away at Christmas,' Naomi suggested, as we sat in her lush back garden, blankets draped over our shoulders, feeling the cold more than James, who was chasing the boys around the garden. 'The boys would love it, and it would be good to get away from all this court stuff.'

'I think that's a great idea,' I replied, sipping my peppermint tea. I had one more court appearance before Christmas. Then we could really concentrate on enjoying our little holiday.

The Children and Family Court Advisory and Support

Service, or CAFCASS, made their first appearance at this hearing.

'CAFCASS are there to represent the voice of the child,' Michelle, my barrister, explained.

I had to go to court alone that day. James had to go to an important business meeting that he couldn't get out of. I took the twenty-minute train journey into Nottingham. As I climbed out of the train, the freezing cold wind hit me. I walked as quickly as I could down to the family court building. Michelle wasn't there. After a few minutes of pacing around the different floors I sat down in a corner of the waiting room. I could feel eyes staring at me from across the room. Glancing up I saw a tall woman, in her mid-forties, at a guess, with a folder in her hands. She didn't look like a solicitor. I took my phone out of my bag and flicked through my newsfeed. Shortly after, Michelle appeared at my side.

'Hi, Mandy, I've got us a meeting room.'

Grabbing my handbag, I followed her through the dimly lit corridors.

'I see CAFCASS have arrived,' she said, glancing over towards the woman who'd been staring at me. 'She'll probably want to speak to you.'

As soon as we sat down Michelle began outlining the day's procedure. She had a slim folder that she kept referring to as she talked me through what she expected to happen. Even though I nodded, I wasn't really taking it in. Like all our conversations, it was punctuated with legal speak that I still didn't fully understand, and I didn't feel inclined to ask questions. I just wanted to be back home, away from all of it. A lady tapped on the window interrupting Michelle's monologue.

'The other advocates want me,' she explained, 'I won't be long.'

I glanced down at the graffiti on the desk below. The words, "evil bastards" had been etched into the wood. There was a knock at the door. I looked up to see the CAFCASS lady's face at the glass, and the door slowly opening.

'Hi, are you Amanda?' She smiled, but her eyes didn't move.

'Yes,' I replied.

'I'm Shirley. You look scared.' She continued smiling. 'There's nothing to be scared of, I don't bite, I promise. Can we talk?'

Yes, of course,' I replied.

Shirley took her jacket off and sat down. Her hair was scraped back into a tight bun, and she wore no make-up. 'Okay so I am the voice of the children. I am what's called a guardian. Here's a leaflet explaining exactly what I do.'

I shoved it in my bag. I already knew the role of the guardian.

'So, I've got a lot of information already from the boy's disclosures, but there is something I'd like to query. Have you ever been abused Amanda?'

'No. Never,' I replied.

'Okay, well, that's all for now. Damian is in the meeting room next door, so I am going to go and speak to him now. But before I do, I would like to arrange with you to visit Lewis and Daniel next Tuesday at five pm? I shall leave you my mobile.' She handed me her card before gathering her bags and striding out of the room in very high stiletto shoes that seemed incongruous with her bare face but at least explained why she was so tall. She paused at the door to give me one last fake smile.

Had I ever been abused? Why would she ask that? What possible relevance could that have?

Seconds later, I heard the familiar tones of Damian's

voice from the other side of the paper-thin wall, and I immediately felt afraid.

Then I heard laughter coming from Shirley. The more laughter coming from him. I covered my ears to block out them both out.

***

I had tidied the house until it was squeaky clean and put away toys that had been resting on the floor for the past month. I even cleaned the windows, though we had them done by a local guy every second Friday. I wanted our place to be perfect. I wanted Shirley to see what a good homemaker I was. A pan of butternut squash soup bubbled away on the hob. I always made homemade soups, that wasn't for show, but I hoped the smell would add to the sense of warmth and cosiness. I wanted Shirley to see how well the boys were cared for. My mum and Naomi had gently mocked my frantic housekeeping reminding me she wasn't a suitor, but a social worker.

I checked the kitchen clock, as the doorbell rang. It was eleven am exactly. She was very punctual. I gave the counter one last wipe, put a lid on the pot of soup and went to let Shirley in.

The boys played on their iPads in the lounge as I led her through and offered her a cuppa.

'Just a glass of water, please,' Shirley replied.

She sat on a stool, sipping the water. She was dressed similar to the day in court. No make-up, extraordinarily high heels.

'You keep the place lovely, Mandy.' She glanced around my neat as a new pin kitchen.

Make sure you write that down, I thought and hated myself for trying so desperately hard to impress this stranger. I wasn't doing it for me, I was doing it for the boys.

Daniel had peered in the door a few times since

Shirley's arrival and decided to brave entering, immediately wrapping his arms around my legs.

'Sweetheart, this is Shirley,' I told him.

'Hi, Daniel, how are you?' Shirley asked, trying to make eye contact.

Daniel smiled shyly. 'Fine, thank you,' he eventually replied, hugging into me tighter.

'Lewis, come and meet Shirley,' I said, shouting so Lewis could hear me.

Seconds later Lewis appeared.

'Oh, you must be Lewis,' said Shirley. 'I've come to have a little chat with you and your brother, if that is okay?'

Lewis glanced at me nervously.

'It's alright, sweetheart, Shirley just wants to have a little talk with you. Why don't you go and show Shirley your new Minecraft figures? I bet she'd love to see those.' I hoped I sounded more enthusiastic than I felt.

Shirley followed Lewis into the lounge. About fifteen minutes later he emerged from their conversation looking flustered and red-cheeked. He cuddled into me, and I placed an arm around him.

'Lewis's been a very good boy,' Shirley said. 'Daniel, can I have a little chat to you now?'

Daniel glanced from Lewis to me then back to Lewis. 'Okay,' he said reluctantly.

After another fifteen minutes Shirley appeared in the kitchen, Daniel behind her. He squeezed past her, rushing over to me, pinning himself to my side.

'Okay, Mandy, I'll be in touch,' she said, as she took her coat and bag. 'Good to meet you boys.'

I heard the front door close. I didn't walk her out as both the boys were clinging to me like a life raft, and I didn't want to let either go. We heard the engine of her car and the sound of her driving off. Lewis ran to the living room window to confirm she was gone.

'Mummy, I don't ever want to see that man again. Is that lady going to make me see him?' He bit his thumbnail anxiously.

He'd taken to calling Madford "that man" only occasionally reverting back to "Dad".

'No, you will never have to see him again, Lewis,' promised my eldest son.

Lewis didn't look convinced. 'I would be so scared if I had to see him again, especially now that we've told.' The pressure was too much for him, and he burst into tears.

'I don't like that lady either, Mummy.' Daniel said. 'She kept asking me the same questions about Daddy.'

'I know, darling.' I ran my fingers through Daniel's hair. 'The lady has to be sure of what you're both saying and that's why she keeps repeating the questions.'

'She asked me what I liked most about "that man",' Lewis told us both. 'And I said, "not seeing him, that's what I like about Dad".'

***

The sudden chill in the air meant that winter was now here. Advent calendars were pinned to the wall and I watched each day disappear in front of me at an alarming rate. The log fire was lit every evening, and in no time at all the shops were filled with Christmas decorations, and we were on our way to a second festive season in our safe and cosy little home. Christmas day was spent at Naomi and James's palatial house. But we had even more exciting plans on Boxing Day.

It was a crisp sunny day when we arrived at the lodge park. As soon as we were shown to our cabins, the boys immediately wanted to get into the hot tub. The whole family spent four adventure packed days cycling, toasting marshmallows in a cabin in the middle of the forest, going to archery and shooting classes and relaxing in the hot tub. The boys were in their element. I gazed at them in the hot tub with their smiling faces and rosy red cheeks. My guys. My precious little guys.

When we had the fact finding out of the way, then we could have more times like these...

Once back at home after the New Year, the stress was tangible. Life carried on as normal in January. The daily routine was still the same. The boys needed minding, the food needed cooking, the house needed to be kept ticking over, but the court case was always at the back of my mind. Looming. Daring me to chill out with my boys and forget about it and then reminding me, like a slap in the face, with another letter, another phone call.

I was in dire need of some new clothes for the fact-finding hearing. I would need to look smart. Being a full-time mum meant that I had given my work suits to charity. Apart from a few glittery tops, my clothes were all casual. I decided to go shopping for appropriate attire. Normally, I love a few hours, alone, in town rooting through racks in search of bargains but buying clothes, especially for court, was different. I resented it, the idea that a fitted suit and matching bag made me a better parent. Michelle had advised that appearance was vital, and I wasn't paying her a small fortune to disregard her suggestions.

'That style really suits you,' a lady trying on jeans enthused about the navy two piece I was gazing absentmindedly at in the communal clock room's full-length mirror. 'A job interview, is it?'

'Something like that,' I replied.

I shoved the last bag into the car and tried not to think about another maxed out credit card. Another few hundred pounds wasn't going to make much difference at this point, but it still bothered me. The cost of this case was endless,

151

but my finances weren't.

**

It was the night before the first day of the hearing at Nottingham family court. With the boys tucked up in bed and the dishes washed, kitchen floor swept, clothes set out for tomorrow, I tried to relax in front of the TV. I flicked between channels until I settled for an episode of *Friends*. But I couldn't relax. Thoughts of court took over completely. I decided to run myself a bath with a few drops of lavender oil. I breathed in the flowery scent and sank into the warm water. *Everything is going to be okay*, I told myself over and over, in the faint hope my mind would believe me.

**

I was sitting opposite my barrister in one of the tiny meeting rooms. My new suit felt tight and restrictive as I crossed and uncrossed my legs and listened to Michelle's instructions.

'Okay, Mandy, so you're first in the witness box. Just answer clearly and honestly. I will start off by asking you to describe the situation and say anything that you feel you need to say. Okay? And then Sebastian Ramsbottom will then be firing questions at you for most of the day. It won't be easy, Mandy, but try to remember it's nothing personal.'

I gave her a weak smile and tried to not to think about the fact that people only every tell you it's not personal when it is.

The others were already seated when I walked in the court room behind my barrister. Madford was sat in the seat, adjacent to my left, with his barrister. Shirley, the CAFCASS guardian, was sitting in the row in front with her solicitor and my barrister. A couple of legal secretaries sat poised ready to type. I look anxiously at the clock. I was too cold to take my coat off. The room felt like it didn't have any central heating, despite it being winter. I shivered, rubbing my hands together. The door to the judge's chambers suddenly swung open, and the usher walked out.

'All rise,' she said in a loud, clear voice.

I clambered to my feet along with everyone else as the judge slid in, his grey hair sleeked back, wearing a smart grey suit and navy blue and white stripy tie with some kind of emblem etched on. He raised his eyebrows and gave a slight smile as he took his seat.

There were the usual formalities, Madford's barrister outlining the case. My barrister agreeing to the outline. A rambling speech about the sensitive nature of family law from the learned judge, and eventually I was in the witness stand.

'Will you be taking an oath on the Bible or without?' the usher asked me.

'The Bible, please.'

The usher handed me the bible. 'Just hold that up in the air,' she said, 'as you read out from this card.'

I took a deep breath and started reading aloud the printed words. 'I swear by almighty God that the evidence I shall give shall be the truth the whole truth and nothing but the truth."

The judge looked at me. 'Miss Taylor, you may take a seat now.'

As soon as I sat down on the cold seat, warm air started to blast out from the vents behind me. I took my coat off, feeling slightly self-conscious as I did. The room was deadly silent, and I was the its sole focus.

Michelle stood up. 'Miss Taylor, why don't you explain to us, in your own words, the lead up to this current court case? Perhaps the events that culminated in your ex-husband, Mr Madford, being arrested and questioned about multiple sexual assaults would be a good place to start.'

I cleared my throat and began on the day my life changed forever when my mum rang to say Lewis and Daniel were being abused by their father. I was certain what Michelle was going to ask and we had practised my testimony. She told me to take my time and to articulate my words slowly and not to be too concerned if I stumbled over details, to keep going. Following her advice, I got through a summary of the worst years of my life in a little over half an hour. She had a few points she wanted to clarify, and then she was finished. Sitting down, she gave me a quick smile.

Sebastian Ramsbottom stood up, peering at me from behind his glasses. 'Miss Taylor, was Mr Madford ever charged for these horrific disclosures of sexual abuse?'

He asked the rhetorical question as if he was genuinely curious. My mouth felt dry, and I reached over to my plastic cup of water, taking a sip. 'No, he wasn't. But then again, the police didn't properly investigate.'

'With the greatest of respect, that's not for you to decide, Miss Taylor,' Ramsbottom replied.

The fluorescent lights flickered. The judge started to speak. 'Miss Taylor, did you believe Lewis when he said he had been sexually abused by his father?' He peered over the top of his glasses.

'Yes, Your Honour, I believed him of course. My son wouldn't lie.'

The judge paused as he scribbled something down with his pen before addressing me once more. 'I have dealt with many rape cases, and it is unusual for the mother to believe her children. Most believe their partner or ex-partner is not capable of raping a child.'

Sebastian Ramsbottom took a minute to ensure the judge was finished before continuing. 'Miss Taylor, please go to File C, and page thirty-four. Paragraph four.'

I looked at the files at my side, sliding out File C and flicked through the pages of the ring binder until I found the right page. It contained a print-out of emails sent between me and Damian in 2010. "You're a pathological liar, Damian. Why do you always lie?"' He read out slowly and deliberately. 'Miss Taylor. What have you got to say about that?'

'I think it was relating to when I asked Damian to leave for a couple of weeks when things were bad between us. It was almost seven years ago. I was pregnant with Daniel and he… things had become pretty bad between us,' I said, failing to see the significance.

Sebastian glanced at the judge who scribbled something down. 'Actually, you're the liar, aren't you, Miss Taylor?' He folded his arms, starting straight at me. 'Miss Taylor, you said that Daniel told you that Mr Madford had drowned him?' he continued. 'Do you seriously think Mr Madford, the man you married, would do that to his own son?' He looked aghast.

'I didn't want to believe it, but I know Daniel wouldn't lie about something like that.'

He rolled his eyes. 'Did it never occur to you, Miss Taylor, that Daniel had a bad dream and that you twisted it into something else in your usual fashion?'

'No!' I shouted.

The judge looked up at me, as if surprised at my raised voice.

'My sons know the difference between a bad dream and reality,' I explained, my voice consciously lower.

'And what about these ridiculous injection allegations against Mr Madford? The boys would have told you if they'd had been injected, wouldn't they? There would have been visible marks. You did it, didn't you? The boys didn't

155

show any emotion in their ABE interview, did they? Because they were making it up for attention. You told them what to say, didn't you, Miss Taylor? Miss Taylor?'

I was speechless.

'Miss Taylor, are you going to answer me or are you going to carry on sitting there ignoring these questions?'

I sat up straighter. The judge peered at me from behind his glasses. 'Are you okay, Miss Taylor?'

'My head hurts,' I heard myself reply.

'Very well, we shall adjourn for five minutes.'

Everyone leapt to their feet as the judge left the room for his chambers. My barrister appeared at the side of me and passed me two paracetamols. 'Thought you might need a couple of these, Mandy.'

I swallowed them with a gulp of water. 'Thanks,' I said. 'I need to use the bathroom.'

Pushing open the lady's toilets I saw Shirley was in there, washing her hands. 'How are the boys, Mandy?' she asked, smiling that same joyless smile.

'To be honest, Shirley, they're not themselves. They're wondering why I am going out every day. And I think they're picking up on the stress of all this.' I blinked back tears; I didn't want Shirley to think I was weak.

'You know the court always act in the best interests of the child, so don't worry,' she said, before exiting the ladies, her high heels tapping noisily against the hard floor.

As soon as she left, I made a beeline for the sink and splashed cold water in my face. Patting my skin dry with a paper towel, I saw the fear screaming in my eyes.

Once back in the court room, the interrogation by Ramsbottom continued. 'Miss Taylor, you say that Lewis struggled to sleep properly at times?'

'Yes, that's right. Whilst he was being abused.'

'So, you thought you would give him sedatives to help

him to sleep, didn't you Miss Taylor? He got too much for you, didn't he?'

'No, *he* drugged my sons!' I pointed to Madford, opposite me, my outstretched hand shaking a little.

The questions continued like a machine gun. By the end of the court day I had been accused of coaching my sons, drugging my sons, manipulating my sons, manipulating my mother and family, manipulating Madford. I had been called vindictive, deranged and neurotic. I had been told Lewis was being home-schooled because I was paranoid about adults harming him, and that Daniel wasn't home-schooled because I couldn't emotionally blackmail him into learning at home. The brutal and relentless questioning by Ramsbottom became too much, and I burst into tears. When my character wasn't being decimated, I was forced to concede points about Madford. Yes, he was a good provider. Yes, the divorce had been amicable, financially. Yes, I had over the years sent him texts and emails thanking him for various parenting tasks. In many ways, Ramsbottom suggested, Madford was a reasonable ex and a good father.

'He raped and drugged his own children,' I retorted.

'To be clear, Miss Taylor, that wasn't my question. Is it fair to say, in many ways, Damian Madford was a reasonable ex and a good father?'

I stared straight ahead.

'Miss Taylor, I need you to answer,' the judge instructed me.

'Once again, Miss Taylor, is it fair to say, in many ways, Damian Madford was a reasonable ex and a good father?'

'Yes,' I croaked.

Eight

It was day two, and Mum's turn in the witness box today. I'd tried to dissuade her from testifying because I couldn't bear for her to be ridiculed in the stand, like I was, even though I was desperate for her words to support the boys' disclosures. She was having none of it.

'It's your job to protect your boys, and it's my job to protect you.'

Glancing over at her now, as she sat opposite Madford, I could tell she was nervous, but she held herself steady, keeping her focus on her hands which she'd placed on her knees. She looked so lovely in her pale pink blouse, her blonde hair immaculate, her make-up subtle and flattering. I'd never been as proud of her.

Michelle led Mum through her testimony, which basically confirmed everything I had already told the court. As a practising counsellor, Mum was confident and articulate and, in my view, came across as very plausible. Michelle's questioning went smoothly with the judge interrupting once to ask Mum why she so certain of particular dates, and Mum explaining that she had kept a diary of events since Lewis had first confided in her.

Michelle sat down, and Sebastian Ramsbottom stood up. Mum stole a quick look at me.

I gave her a reassuring smile.

'Thank you for coming today, Ms Roberts,' Ramsbottom began. 'The court and my client appreciate your time.' He paused and took a sip of water. '"I know you're a very…' he paused again 'involved grandparent and that you've spent a great deal of time looking after them.'

'Those boys are my world. It's a pleasure to care for them,' Mum replied. She was speaking to Ramsbottom but looking at me.

'"Your World",' Ramsbottom repeated, 'and I have no difficulty believing you would do anything for them?'

'I would,' Mum confirmed.

'Including lie for them, if you thought it was in their best interests?'

Mum didn't answer, and I could see that she was shocked at his suggestion. Ramsbottom continued, 'You live alone, Miss Roberts?'

'Yes,' Mum agreed.

'And are single?' he asked her.

Mum didn't answer him, like she was confused at the question.

'Is this relevant?' the judge directed his question at Ramsbottom.

'I believe it will help shed light on Miss Roberts's motivations,' Ramsbottom explained to the judge.

The judge nodded.

'Miss Roberts, you must answer the question,' he instructed Mum.

'Yes, I'm single.' Mum told the court.

'So, you're a single divorcee of somewhat advanced years,' Ramsbottom paused and appeared embarrassed to have point out Mum's age, 'perhaps lonely, certainly devoted to your grandchildren. Perhaps unhealthily so?'

Though spoke like questions, Ramsbottom was making statements. 'You're obsessed with paedophiles aren't you, Ms Roberts?' This time it was a question,

'No,' my mum said.

Poor Mum getting harassed by a privately educated bully.

'Lewis was clearly messing around. He wasn't disclosing sexual abuse. He was just trying to get your attention, wasn't he?'

'No. He was telling the truth about his horrific abuse,' Mum said. Though she kept her voice low, she glared at Madford.

Sebastian Ramsbottom shook his head. 'I think you're lying, Ms Roberts! It's all one big lie, isn't it?'

'I am not lying. I'm telling the truth.' Mum was starting to sound exasperated.

I looked over at the judge. *Surely, he should be stepping in?*

'This is all a fiction, isn't it, Ms Roberts? You coached the boys into making disclosures about their father, his family and friends, didn't you?'

'No, of course not. The boys came to me. Why would I do something like that?'

Ramsbottom ignored the question. 'Then why didn't they tell you sooner, Ms Roberts?' he asked her.

'Lewis told us that his daddy would constantly threaten him with, "if you tell anyone then you'll never see Mummy again."'

'Oh, shut up, Ms Roberts! Have you ever thought about the emotional consequences of the boys not seeing their father for two years?'

'Once we found out what their father was doing, our only thoughts have been for the welfare of the boys. The negative consequences of seeing him were so obviously outweighed any positive ones. In any event, they have blossomed since they haven't seen their father. They were all over the place a couple of years ago. Now they are like different children. They have improved drastically because of his absence.'

Good old Mum! Explaining basic child welfare to the experts.

'Ms Roberts, I watched the boys' ABE interviews, and none of them showed any emotion when describing the alleged abuse by their father, isn't that unusual?' The question came from the judge.

'Your Honour, I'm a qualified counsellor. In my experience, this is what both adults and children do when describing their abuse. They have to dissociate in order to be able to keep going. They function by shutting off from the emotion when describing the abuse. It's a coping mechanism. With children, it is even more complex because they don't fully grasp the concept of time so they have even less context for what has happened.'

'Thank you for that clarification, Miss Roberts,' the judge said, then nodded his head to indicate Ramsbottom could continue.

The lights flickered. I glanced over at the wall with its peeling paint and a dated picture, probably a few decades old, of a beach scene. It had faded over time and now appeared as depressed as the room it hung in.

'You helped plan this entire charade, didn't you, Ms Roberts? So that you and your daughter could raise the children without a father? You should be utterly ashamed of yourself.'

'No,' Mum protested, 'It was nothing like…'

Ramsbottom interrupted with his next question. 'You've already explained that your job as a councillor means you have a professional understanding of paedophilia. That's where the idea to accuse the boy's father of incest came from, isn't it?

'No, goodness, no.' Mum's voice sounded strained.

'You both wanted to make sure Mr Madford was deprived access to his children. You ordered the drugs off the internet and gave them to the boys, didn't you?'

'No,' Mum said quietly.

'Because Mr Madford never sexually abused either Lewis or Daniel, did he?' Ramsbottom asked.

'He did,' Mum replied, but she sounded defeated.

I shook my head. I was furious. *Why had Michelle and the judge allowed my mother to be harassed like that?* She was performing her civic duty; she wasn't a criminal. I looked up to see Madford smirking as he leaned back into his chair.

Hours later, with the kids in bed, I was still seething. I sipped a glass of wine and went over the day's events in my head. As I recalled Ramsbottom's rapid fire questions and Mum's reluctant answers I realised the significance of what Madford's barrister had said. *"You ordered the drugs off the internet and gave them to the boys, didn't you?"* Madford was going to say we drugged the boys.

My poor mum was attacked in the witness box for another two whole days. By the end of it, she had the migraine from hell. Ramsbottom had been so relentless in his false accusations, continual questioning and name calling, that the judge finally called for an end to the gruelling twenty-hour ordeal.

Naomi and James were the final witnesses for our side. They were both subjected to the same set of farcical questions as Mum and I had been, but thankfully for much less time. Their combined evidence took us up to three pm Friday, after which the judge decided to call time for the first week.

'These proceedings are never easy,' he said in a paternal

tone. 'Ordinary people with no previous experience of the courts find themselves having to speak about the personal and intimate details of their lives and having to sit and listen as allegations and counter allegations are bandied about. To that end, I'd like to congratulate both parties and all concerned for getting through the first week. Court will reconvene at ten am on Monday.'

'All rise,' the usher ordered us as the judge stood up and headed back to his chambers.

"Counter Allegations," hearing the phrase again, I shuddered. At least I knew what it meant this time…

***

Week two began wet and miserable, in perfect synchrony with my own emotions. DC Webster and DI Wright were pencilled in for Monday, and I felt sick to the stomach at the thought of what lay ahead.

'Try not to worry,' Michelle whispered to me, as we sat waiting for Webster to be sworn.

I gave her a weak smile.

After he took his oath, Webster caught my eye and winked. I glanced at Michelle, to see if she had noticed, but she was quietly whispering to the CAFCASS solicitor.

Sebastian Ramsbottom was the first to address Webster. 'DC Webster, I am counsel for the father. How did Mr Madford cooperate during the investigation?'

'He cooperated fully with our investigation. He was polite and handed over his phone and laptop.' Webster replied.

'Would you say that you acted in a biased way towards Mr Madford?' Sebastian Ramsbottom continued.

'No, not at all. I acted in an unbiased way, at all times, abiding by the police codes of conduct.'

No, you didn't, you liar!

'Are you happy with your role in the investigation into

the allegations brought by Miss Taylor against Mr Madford?' Ramsbottom continued.

'The investigation was carried out thoroughly and efficiently.'

His reply was so practised, he began speaking before the question was finished.

'Thank you, DC Webster, that's all.'

Ramsbottom sat down.

Michelle did a quick check of the notes she'd scrawled on her pad and stood up.

'Mr Webster, Miss Taylor stated that you made some very inappropriate comments during your second meeting with her. You said that "you can tell what a paedophile looks like, and Mr Madford isn't one", you also said "children say these things when their parent's divorce". What have you got to say about that?'

'I don't recall saying any of those things, perhaps Miss Taylor is confused, she was clearly very stressed when I spoke with her. But what I will say is that Mr Madford came across as innocent, it was as if he didn't have anything to hide.' He directed these comments at the judge.

Michelle continued. 'What about the email to DCI Montford in which you state, regarding the drugs results, "boss, here's the report, doesn't change a great deal, but she will make a big deal of it."?'

DC Webster shrugged and mumbled something inaudible.

'I'm sorry, Mr Webster, I didn't quite hear that, could you repeat that please?'

'I found Miss Taylor to be quite hysterical and not that credible. I guess this email reflects that.' His voice was quieter than previous comments.

'But Lewis disclosed that his father had injected him, then the hair analysis indicates the presence of a number of date rape drugs. I would suggest that IS indeed a big deal?' Michelle said.

'I just meant that it still doesn't prove how the children ended up with drugs in their hair. It may have been surface contamination.'

Surface Contamination, I scrolled the words on the front of the pad Michelle had given me. *What did that even mean?*

Madford smirked and leaned further back into his chair.

'Finally, Mr Webster, did you carry out a full house search at Mr Madford's?

'No, it wasn't necessary. All we needed was his phone and laptop, as I say, which he handed over.'

'So, despite both boys having disclosed that they had been drugged, you didn't see any reason to search the house for drugs and drug paraphernalia?'

'Had we found anything questionable on either his phone or laptop, we would have done so,' Webster replied.

After lunch it was DI Karen Wright in the witness box. She sat perfectly still, waiting to be sworn in. This was the first time I had ever seen her. She had highlighted hair, cold eyes and pointy features. She was probably in her early fifties.

Sebastian Ramsbottom stood up. 'DI Wright, how long have you been a serving police officer?'

'Twenty-five years,' she barked in her harsh Northern Irish twang.

'How many child sex abuse investigations have you carried out?'

'Countless. There are too many to name,' she said proudly.

'Can you give us a summary as to the investigation you carried out into the allegations brought by Miss Taylor about Mr Madford?'

'Yes, arrests were made, interviews were carried out, devices were seized. A thorough investigation was done.

'And what did you conclude?' he asked.

'The boys wanted to please their mum and grandma and they knew how to do this. They were given a book about sex abuse so they didn't know the difference between real life and pretend. I have never been as concerned about two children as I have about these boys. The disclosures were fantastical, injections, groups of men. It doesn't sound real. Mr Madford presents well. He seems like a good decent man. This will have no doubt had a detrimental effect not only on the boys, but on Mr Madford, who is clearly the victim in all of this.'

I glanced at Madford. He was affecting a sad pose as if to suggest all this was hard on him.

'Thank you, Miss Wright. I have no further questions.'

Michelle gave Wright a smile before beginning. 'Thank you for your time, Miss Wright. My first question is why would you say that the boy's disclosures were fantastical? Aren't Rochdale Police the same police force that failed miserably with the grooming scandal?

'Yes, in that case, mistakes have been made but lessons have been learned,' Wright conceded.

Michelle continued, 'Children were abused by groups of men? Children were drugged by groups of men?'

'Yes,' Wright replied.

'So, why did you describe Lewis and Daniel's disclosures as fantastical?'

'It just didn't sound real, that's all. And to be honest they were very young children, who can often get mixed up with what is real and what is imagined.'

'But, Ms Wright, the boys were telling the truth. And now the hair analysis indicates the presence of date rape drugs.'

'That's true, but we don't know how they got there. They could have been picked up of worktops.'

Worktops? What did that even mean? I scrawled the word *worktops* next to *surface contamination* on my notepad.

'Finally, Miss Wright, have you ever met Miss Taylor and her sons?'

'No.'

After the questioning had finished for the day, Michelle indicated for me to meet her in the waiting room. 'I tried, Mandy, but those police, wow, what is their problem?' She looked as defeated as I felt.

'Why were they talking about surface contamination and workshops? What does that mean?' I asked.

'They're clutching at straws, trying to find alternative explanations for the hair samples. It's to be expected, they have to say something.'

'But the judge will see right through it, won't he?'

Michelle paused before replying, 'Let's hope so, eh?'

As James and I walked back to the carpark in silence we passed a café and I saw the silhouette of Webster and Wright sat in the window. I stopped in my tracks and watched as DI Wright stroked DC Webster's cheek. He smiled and leaned into her, whispering something in her ear.

That evening after the boys were bathed and ready for bed, I poured myself glass of red wine and squeezed onto the sofa between them to watch an episode of, *You've Been Framed.* It was part of our nightly routine. The boys each had a cup of warm milk. It was a perfect end to an awful day. A tear streamed down my cheek as Lewis and Daniel giggled at the tv show.

The next day started with Doctor Sullivan was in the witness box. She almost blended into the wall with her mousy hair, beige clothes and transparent glasses.

As usual, Sebastian Ramsbottom was the first to address the witness. 'Dr Sullivan, can you please tell us about the disease that caused scaring on Lewis' buttocks and anus?'

I flinched. I hated that a room full of strangers were listening to my son's private medical details.

'Mollscum contagiosum can be passed from child to child through sharing towels,' Dr Sullivan explained.

My GP in Littleborough's words rang through my mind, *"I would always inform parents that it can be sexually transmitted if it's contracted in the genital or anal area."*

'You took hair samples of the boys? Are you aware that a number of sedatives were found in the boy's hair?'

'No, I didn't know that.' She glanced at me, and I could see a flash of guilt in her eyes.

Good! She should feel guilty. They all should.

'Dr Sullivan, did you notice any signs that the boys had been subjected to gang rape?'

'Daniel refused to have his pants taken down, and I only checked Lewis externally. But I was informed that the last contact with the father had taken place five weeks prior to our appointment. We suggest sexual health checks are carried out within two weeks. Children's bodies heal very quickly plus abuse, such as oral rape, cannot be detected on medical examinations.' She cleared her throat before adding, 'If children are drugged, then this will mean tearing is less likely.'

If Ramsbottom was annoyed at how the questioning was going, he didn't show it. 'It is ridiculous, wouldn't you say, Dr Sullivan, that Mr Madford is alleged to have gang raped a three-year-old and seven-year-old, and they don't have any physical signs of tearing?'

'No, most children don't have tears, especially after two weeks, and I didn't get to examine Daniel because…'

'That's enough, thank you, Dr Sullivan, no further questions,' Sebastian Ramsbottom interrupted.

'I have no questions for the witness,' Michelle told the court.

That afternoon, after we had returned from the lunch break, a representative from Alore Forensics—the company that carried out the testing of the hair samples—Kirsty Thomas, took the stand. She had straight, lank, dyed orange hair and was chewing her nails.

Ramsbottom rose from his seat. 'Ms Thomas, can these drugs be injected?' he asked, getting straight to the point.

'Yes, Zolpidem can be injected. I think the benzodiazepines can be injected, but I'm not too sure. It's not really my field.' She scrunched up her nose slightly, then looked quickly down as if she was uncomfortable.

'Could these drugs be picked up from contaminated worktops?' he asked.

'Yes, it could be surface contamination, I suppose,' she replied, shrugging.

She sounded more like a moody teenager than our star witness, and I could have cried.

'How much should you give to a child for it to show up on a hair strand test?' Ramsbottom asked.

What a strange way to phrase the question.

'I'm not sure,' she replied. 'There is no research on children with these types of drugs.'

'Thank you, Ms Thomas,' Ramsbottom said, before taking his seat.

'Miss Thomas,' Michelle began, 'can you tell us when the boys had been administered the drugs that were found in their hair and the likely time of exposure?'

'It's difficult to tell on children' she replied.

It's very easy to tell! What's wrong with you?

169

'What is the average hair growth rate?' Michelle asked.

Thank God for Michelle!

'Well, its roughly one centimetre per month, but children's hair is variable.'

'So, taking that growth rate into account, then for Daniel, for example, whose hair sample measured seven centimetres, would that equate roughly to drugs being administered regularly in his hair during the seven months before the hair samples were taken?' she asked.

'Yes, that's right,' she replied.

***

Then I was back at home kissing my babies goodnight in their beds after quickly catching up with them about their days. Then I was awake staring at the ceiling till the small hours. Then it was morning. Getting ready for court, Mum picking up the boys, James picking me up. Then I was sat in the court room, Michelle by my side.

It was Shirley Milton, the guardian, in the witness box today. She appeared relaxed and composed. I prayed a silent prayer that she would present favourably in her evidence. She had met Lewis and Daniel after all. She could see that they were telling the truth.

'Either the boys have been sexually abused, or they believe that they have been sexually abused but haven't,' she said when Michelle asked her what she had concluded.

My jaw almost hit the floor. *Why on earth would any child believe they had been sexually abused if they hadn't?*

I was barely aware of the rest of her evidence. I caught snippets as my head reeled.

'I do have concerns about the book *The Right Touch* and how it could have negatively influenced the boys.'

It was a stranger danger book! There was nothing in there about being raped and drugged! Who IS this woman?

'I do not have any thoughts as to who administered the

drugs or how they arrived in the boy's systems, safe that I am extremely concerned about that.'

'I leave it to Your Honour to decide how they ended up in the boy's hair.'

'I did find the mother to be an incredibly anxious woman.'

You'd be anxious too, if your children were being raped! I'd allowed this woman into my home. I'd told both my boys to trust her and tell her the truth.

'I don't like that lady, Mummy.' Wasn't that what Daniel had said? *Out of the mouths of babes…*

***

'Why do you have to keep going out all day, Mummy?' Lewis asked that evening as the three of us snuggled up on the sofa.

'It's just boring work stuff,' I lied. 'It'll be over with soon. Only a couple more days sweetheart.' I ruffled his hair.

I sensed that he knew I wasn't being honest.

The following morning as I arrived in court, I saw the familiar outline of a group of men huddled together in the waiting area. Jeremy Green, dressed in a tweed suit and brief case immediately spotted me and smiled, lifting up his hand to wave. Shivering, I quickly raced towards the meeting room where Michelle was waiting.

'Are you okay, Mandy?'

'No. I feel sick. I just saw them all outside.'

Michelle gave me a reassuring smile. 'Yes, we have a few of them in the witness box today. I'll try to get through them pretty quick.' She handed me a glass of water. 'Drink this and then we're going to have to go in.'

'I swear to tell the truth, the whole truth and nothing but the truth.' Green's voice sounded as arrogant as I remembered.

'Mr Green, I'm counsel for the father, how long have you known Lewis and Daniel?' Ramsbottom began.

'All their lives,' Green replied. 'Although I haven't seen them since the…' he paused, 'since their mother made false allegations involving her ex-husband, my partner and me, and God knows how many others. It's not right that she can get away with this.' He glared at me, and I pictured how his evil face must have terrified my sons, with his bald head and forehead etched with a deep scar.

'How has this affected your life, Mr Green?'

'It's caused so much stress. You know, Mandy and I used to be friends, at one time, we used to all socialise together. It's just so sad that it's come to this.' He looked at me again, this time with pity.

'Finally, Mr Green, and I apologise for the directness of my question, have you ever sexually abused Lewis and Daniel Madford?'

'Never. Everything she has said is lies. She must have trained the kids well. She is a very damaged woman.' He looked at the judge as he spoke.

'Thank you, that is all,' Ramsbottom concluded.

Michelle stood up. 'Mr Green, in your police interview you state that you hardly ever saw the boys. That you hadn't seen them for three-four-five years. But you go on to describe Lewis's character. Why is this?'

I could see tiny beads of sweat breaking trickling down his bald head. 'Well, sometimes one can lose track of time, and yes, you can sometimes forget certain gatherings that you have attended, as I am sure everyone in this room has done.'

'Your husband, Mr Wood, said something very different in his police interview. He said that you had both last seen Lewis and Daniel at a picnic just a couple of months before your arrest.'

'Yes, well, that's an easy mistake for him to make. He was getting mixed up with another child, friend of the family.' He smiled. 'We may be gay men, but we live very conventional lives and a lot of our circle have children.'

The judge looked up and gave a slight nod.

'You regularly have young rent boys over for sex, don't you, Mr Green?'

'My husband and I enjoy an open marriage. I don't see that this has any relevance.'

'Not so conventional then?' Michelle quipped.

'Keep it relevant, Ms Moore,' the judge cautioned.

'Mr Green, Lewis described you and your husband doing some "bad things" to him, such as "hitting him all over his body", he also said that you "hit his willy" and "did bad things to his bottom".'

'That is totally false. I have never done such a thing. I have always got on well with the boys.' He turned again to the judge. This time his face was pleading.

'Mr Green, in your police interview you say that you hadn't seen Lewis for three-four-five years, so, can I clarify that when you say that you have always got on well with the boys, taking into account Daniel's age at the time which was three years old, then you wouldn't have ever met him?'

'Well, I can explain that, with the passage of time and so on and so forth, and seeing and meeting up with various friends with children and gatherings, it can be easy to become confused as to who you have seen, and these scenarios roll into one another, and you are left with life itself, which difficult to place into specific time categories. I have never been good at pinning things and people down to certain time frames.'

What kind of answer was that? Answer the damn question!

'Mr Green, that will be all. Thank you.' Michelle sat back down.

'Thank you, Your Honour. And apologies, I have a tendency to be fairly verbose,' Green said before leaving the witness stand.

The judge gave him a slight smile.

Next in the witness box was Bill Madford. He looked older and weaker than I remembered but he still had his toad-like hooded eyes. When he spoke, it was in his husky, west country twang. 'I haven't been able to see my grandsons for over two years,' he croaked. 'It's made both me and my wife ill. It's all a load of rubbish. Anyone with any ounce of sense can see that. That woman sat over there, and her family, are an utter disgrace.' He pointed a shaky hand at me spitting out the last sentence.

The judge paused from taking his notes, momentarily glancing toward Bill Madford and nodding.

'He can't do that,' I whispered to Michelle. 'He's as good as said he believes him.'

'Try not to worry,' Michelle whispered back. 'He does that with everybody.'

But he didn't. He didn't nod in agreement with me or with Mum or with James or with Naomi. Nope. He was very selective who he nodded in agreement with.

After lunch Stan Lee took the stand. He was unshaven, and though wearing a suit, it had neither been washed nor pressed. Like the previous witnesses, he denied everything, even knowing the boys.

'They were the kids of a band member. To be honest, I didn't even know either of their names. I mean I might have met them, socially, sure, but only in a big group situation, and off the top of my head, I can't even think when.'

'It must have come as a shock, then, to find yourself accused of sexually assaulting both boys?' Ramsbottom asked.

174

'Yes,' Lee agreed. 'It literally made no sense then Damian explained to me that things were really bad between him and Amanda, and that she'd stop at nothing to hurt him. Even still, it's so extreme.'

'How has this ordeal impacted on you, Mr Lee? It can't be easy to be accused of such a shocking crime.'

'It's affected my job, my mental health, I had to be signed off, and I was too ashamed to tell the doctor what had happened, my home life, everything. It's the worst thing a human being can be accused of, isn't it?' He appealed to Ramsbottom.

'It is,' Madford's council agreed. 'It certainly is.'

Michelle tried to dent his certainty that he barely knew the boys but wound up making him sound even more credible.

'No further questions,' she declared, after asking only a couple.

***

I read to Daniel first. 'Which books do you want tonight, darling?' I helped him into his pyjamas.

'The glow in the dark one. I love that one, Mummy'

'Okay, let's make the room nice and dark then. You get into bed, sweetheart.'

Daniel quickly got into his lower bunk and under the covers. I took the book off the shelf, closed the door and felt my way through the pitch-black room. I pulled out my mobile phone, shining the torch onto the pages in the book to activate the glow in the dark sea creatures. Then I pulled the duvet over us both as I climbed in with Daniel. We both giggled. Daniel never failed to be delighted in seeing the lit-up jellyfish, squid and lantern fishes. We lay like this for about ten minutes.

'Shall I read about the creatures now?'

'Yes, Mummy! I want you to read about the shark and

the octopus.'

Daniel proudly told me the name of each one as I showed him the page.

'Okay, it's time for sleep now. Give me a hug.'

My precious boy snuggled up in my arms, I breathed in the scent of his freshly washed hair and stroked his soft cheek with the back of my hand. I didn't want this moment to end. 'I love you so much, Daniel.'

'I love you more than all the stars in the sky, Mummy.'

'And I love you more than all the rainbows and all the stars and the entire universe,' I replied.

'Mummy don't forget the Lord's prayer,' Daniel said sleepily.

'Of course, sweetheart.'

I stroked Daniel's hair, and together we recited the Lord's prayer. It had been part of our nightly routine for the past few months.

Putting some gentle music on my phone to help him fall asleep, I crept quietly out of his bedroom and into mine, where Lewis was patiently waiting, with the cat curled up next to him.

'Look at you two,' I sighed, ruffling my son's hair as I climbed into the bed next to him.

'Mummy, she's just so cute.' He smiled, stroking Molly as she stood up and stretched, before climbing up onto Lewis's pillow and curling up next to his head. Lewis giggled as I picked up the book next to me. *Wild Horse Island*, it was called. I started reading. After a few minutes, Lewis started giggling.

'Mummy, Molly's nibbling my head!' he exclaimed. 'It tickles!'

'Molly, you naughty little cat.'

Once Molly had settled down, I managed to finish the rest of the chapter.

'Mummy, can I sleep in your room?' Lewis widened his eyes.

'No, you're going into your room, sweetheart,' I said, gently.

'Okay, but can you come and lie down with me for a bit, Mummy?'

'Of course,' I said, following him into his room, where sleeping Daniel lay on the bottom bunk, gently snoring.

Tomorrow, Madford was in the witness box, I wasn't going to sleep a wink.

Nine

I had got up earlier than usual and spent longer on my appearance than any of the previous days. Make-up was the closest thing to armour I had, and I needed to look my strongest if I was going to face him. Satisfied that I'd done my best, I headed downstairs where my already excitable children were helping themselves to cereal.

'We're making breakfast, Mummy,' Daniel squealed with delight.

I sighed at the sight of spilt milk and scattered cornflakes as Lewis missed the aim on both counts. My mum was on it, wiping down the table with one hand and gathering up the flakes with the other. She had insisted on staying last night so she could help this morning.

'You look really pretty, Mummy,' Lewis declared. 'Is there a special day in work?'

'Something like that,' I replied.

Michelle's face appeared concerned as we sat waiting for proceedings to kick off. The judge had entered, Ramsbottom had called Madford and an usher was swearing him in.

'I swear to tell the truth, the whole truth and nothing but the truth, so help me God.' Madford spoke clearly but quietly.

'You wouldn't know the truth if it hit you across the face!' I wanted to scream, *'and you'll never know God!'*

'Mr Madford, you may be seated,' the judge instructed him.

Sebastian Ramsbottom rose to his feet, slowly. He spoke deliberately and softly. 'Mr Madford, can you tell the court about the relationship that you once had with your sons?'

Madford paused, looked wistfully at the judge and cleared his throat before answering,

'Yes, we were a close unit, we had so much fun together. I used to love having them to stay at mine. It was great. They were good boys.'

'And how has Miss Taylor's allegations made you feel, Mr Madford?' Ramsbottom asked.

'Well, we, just totally in shock, really. I don't know where she gets these things from. She needs help, bless her. We used to be in love and stuff at one time, you know.'

I need help! You're the one raping kids! Could anyone else see this fake display? I looked around the room, unable to read expressions.

'Mr Madford, have you ever been arrested for anything up until Ms Taylor's accusations?'

Madford cleared his throat, looking up at his barrister.

'No, not at all. I have never been arrested for anything in my life up until that utter nonsense.'

He reached forward, picked up a cup of water and took a sip.

'How long were you and Ms Taylor in a relationship for?'

'Eight years. I thought they were good years, I never

179

expected her to do anything like this,' Madford's eyes started to glisten.

You're a liar! A liar! A Liar!

'Do you need five minutes?' Ramsbottom feigned concern.

'No, I'll keep going. Best to get it over with.' Madford looked at the judge.

'Are you in a long-term relationship now, Mr Madford?' Ramsbottom took the briefest of glances at his notepad.

'Yes, I certainly am. I am very lucky to say that I have a lovely girlfriend. She's amazing. All the more so for putting up with me.' He laughed, a forced laughed, which abruptly stopped after a couple of seconds.

'Does your long-term girlfriend have any children?'

'Yes, she does, a boy and a girl. Teenagers. They're great kids.'

Ramsbottom paused, looking at the judge, until the judge met his eyes.

'How would you and your sons typically spend time together? What would you do together as a family?'

'We would do lots of fun and stuff, like playing with toys and watching a good film on TV, going cycling in the park, that kind of stuff.'

He smiled shyly.

You liar! You drugged and raped them! You terrified them!

'No further questions, Thank you Mr Madford.'

Ramsbottom took a seat, the slightest of smirks betraying his otherwise stoic look.

Madford crossed his arms behind his head and leaned back into his chair. Michelle stood up and turned to face him

'Mr Madford, going back over two years, why did your sons never want to spend time with you? Why would they kick up such a fuss, crying and screaming, whenever you collected them?'

Madford shook his head, 'I don't know, I honestly had no idea why they behaved like that. They were always okay once they got to mine, though.'

No, they weren't okay! You attacked my sons! You terrorised them!

He looked away, as if to hurry Michelle on to the next question.

'Did your father abuse you?'

'No. That's utter rubbish.' He snorted and glanced downwards.

'Well that's not what you told Lewis is it, Mr Madford? You told Lewis that "Granddad Bill did it to me when I was a little boy and gave me sweets afterwards" didn't you?'

Madford looked furious for a split second then regaining his composure, he looked straight at Michelle.

'No, of course I didn't say that. I don't know where that came from.'

'What about the injections Mr Madford? Why did you drug your sons?'

'I didn't drug my sons. I have no idea where the drugs have come from.'

He was keeping a calm veneer but I could tell Michelle was rattling him.

'Lewis said, very clearly, in his ABE interview that you injected him. He kept saying that you did this to him. Are you saying that your son is lying?'

Well done Michelle!

'No, of course not, but maybe he's confused. His mother has confused him with her nonsense.'

The judge paused and peered down at Madford, scribbling something on his court papers.

'Mr Madford, I'd like you to turn to File D, page

twenty-eight.' Michelle continued.

Madford turned a few pages until he stopped at a page. He raised his eyebrow slightly, as he studied the page.

'Found it.' He said.

'Mr Madford, you'll recognise this as being some of your web searches from October 2014?'

Michelle paused.

'I can explain that.' He spoke quickly.

'Mr Madford, with all due respect, please wait for the question,' Michelle replied.

'Sorry, yes of course.'

'Mr Madford, you searched for Manchester Teen Escort Duos. Look at the time stamp. It was 3pm on a Wednesday afternoon.'

'I was just looking,' he sounded contrite.

'Mr Madford look at the previous week. Please turn to the previous page. Same time, Wednesday afternoon you type in "Manchester Teen Escort Duos" again, Mr Madford.'

'Just having a look,' he repeated.

Liar. You wanted to have sex with teenagers.

'Mr Madford, you said that your current partner has teenage children?'

'Yes, a boy and girl,' he answered.

'We already know that,' Michelle cut in. 'Do you go to see teenage prostitutes, Mr Madford?'

'No, no, no, I was curious, that's all.'

Each reply was fainter.

'How do you think your current partner would respond to this? She has two teenagers. How old would they have been when you first started seeing her?'

The judge suddenly interjected.

'I don't think Mr Madford needs to answer that question, can we move on please?'

Michelle appeared unphased by the judge's sudden interruption.

'Please turn to page thirty-one, Mr Madford.'

The room was silent for about twenty seconds, aside from all the advocates and the judge quietly leafing through their files and tablets.

'Got it.' He said.

'You'll see at 1:33pm you googled the news story about Ian Watkins from the band Lost Prophets. I have the exact news story here for all who don't know who he is. "The rock singer Ian Watkins has received a thirty-five-year sentence, after admitting a string of sex offences involving children including the attempted rape of a baby. The South Wales Police investigation into Watkins codenamed "Operation Globe", required the co-operation of GCHQ to decrypt a hidden drive on his laptop, which was found to contain video evidence of his abuses." Then you'll see at 1:36pm, Mr Madford, that you immediately googled a porn site called "You Jizz" opening another tab, so you could keep referring back to the story about Ian Watkins. Why were you doing that Mr Madford? You were clearly very aroused by those stories about child rape, weren't you?"

'No, not at all. Not at all.' He shrugged his shoulders.

'Were you masturbating, Mr Madford?'

'No. I was just reading and thinking about women, that's all. I just fancy women, that's all. Can't remember really it was ages ago. But I don't do that anymore, I think I must have been feeling a bit down.'

Madford looked at Ramsbottom, who gave him a reassuring nod.

'Because you have a pattern of reading these type of news stories and then going straight onto a porn site. You were clearly aroused by what you read, Mr Madford, so much so that you went straight to a porn site so you could masturbate.' Michelle flicked through her notes. 'There are many others I could refer to. More stories of children and babies being raped and tortured and then the same pattern of you immediately going to a porn site such as "You Jizz" or "UK Perv".'

'That's quite enough, please,' the judge interrupted Michelle again, 'I think we have the idea.'

I could see Michelle calculate the risk of continuing and deciding against it. I was disappointed as we had dozens more examples of his perversion, but I conceded she was probably right. There was no point in disobeying the judge and he'd already said, "I think we have the idea."

'No further questions,' Michelle took her seat.

'Very well, you may step down, Mr Madford,' the judge instructed.

'Your Honour, if I may redirect?' Sebastian Ramsbottom spoke suddenly.

The normally controlled Michelle swore under her breath.

'What's wrong?' I whispered.

'He's going to have the last word,' she hissed back.

Having been granted permission to ask another question, Ramsbottom was enjoying his moment.

'Mr Madford, so much of this trial has focused on the hyperbolic allegations of your ex-wife, accusations that have been refuted by yourself and your co-accusers, the police and the CPS,' he took a minute, making sure every word had sunk in to his audience of one, the judge. 'My question to you is quite muted, mundane even, compared to Miss Taylor's lurid claims, but none the less, it is a very important question.' He paused again.

The impressive built up meant we were all on the edge of our seat in expectation of a big reveal.

'Do you miss them, Mr Madford? Do you miss your

two sons?'

The simplicity of his question was like a kick in the stomach, and Madford's contrived answer was like a second kick in the head.

'Every minute of every day,' Madford's voice faltered. 'I keep thinking what they'll look like by now, I don't get any photos.'

That's because you're a sick paedophile!

'I keep these, Your Honour.' Madford had switched his focus from his barrister to the judge. He had taken his wallet from his pocket and was leafing through it, until he found a photo. I couldn't see it clearly, but it wasn't for my eyes. He handed it to the judge, who seemed slightly embarrassed as he glanced at it and returned it to Madford.

'If you had one hope, regarding the outcome of this hearing, what would it be?' Ramsbottom asked.

What kind of question is that? He's already said what he wants from the hearing. That's literally why we're having a hearing…

'I just want to see my son's faces,' Madford's personal plea was seeking a lot less than his legal plea. 'Your Honour,' he once again stared straight at the judge. 'Children need fathers.'

Ten

27th March 2017

'Where are we going Mummy?' Lewis asked.

I glanced at him through the rear-view mirror of the car I've hired. Lewis looked pale. He could sense something was very wrong. Suffering severe abuse had made him hyper vigilant.

'Just on a little holiday, that's all,' I replied, my words came out rapidly. 'Sorry, sweetheart, I can't really talk. I've got a bad headache and I'm trying to concentrate on the driving.' I added.

The second part was true. My morning in court had ended dramatically. I was planning to be in court until lunch-time. Michelle had said that the judgements were long and convoluted and often took several hours. Because I walked out within twenty minutes, I can't answer to the veracity of her claims. I did not see it coming until it was too late and his words, like a train crash, were derailing the only family life my children had ever known.

"I find the Mother to be irretractable in her conviction

that her children were victims of abuse..." That's a lot of fancy words for the statement, "She believes her children", only that wasn't what he was trying to say. He was blaming me, for all of it, saying that my belief was "unfounded but strongly held". *Unfounded. How could he say that?* I showed him why I thought it, the boys showed him. He watched them both bare their soul in their police interviews in a desperate attempt to be heard and then he says that the abuse allegations had no foundations?

'Mummy, I need a wee!' Lewis sounded almost apologetic.

Looking out over the open road ahead, I judged we were twenty minutes from a petrol station. 'Can you wait a little while?' I asked.

'Okay, Mummy, but not too long!' He scrunched up his face then let it relax again.

'Why don't you sing a song with your brother?' I suggested. *That would take his mind of a wee.*

'I don't want to sing! It will make me think of weeing!' Lewis retorted.

I wasn't about to have an argument, so I shuffled around my bag until I found one of two brand-new iPads and handed it to him. I had planned to give them each one as a gift, when the court case was behind us. Now, that idea seemed fortuitous because I'd left my own mobile at home, with my car. I knew I was being paranoid. *How hard were they going to look for a mum and her little boys?* But I'd never done anything like this before, and I was pretty sure cars and phones were the easiest to track.

The sat nav was telling me where to go next, and I tried to keep focussed, but my head was pounding. All I could hear were the words of the judge going round and around in my mind. I checked the time. It was one-thirty. If we stopped for the bathroom and picked up some snacks and groceries, we would still be at the lodge in under an hour.

I still couldn't believe I was doing this, running away with my kids, like a common criminal, but what choice did I have? What had the judge called me – *irrational?* Which is court speak for crazy. *How could he call me crazy?* I've never experienced mental ill health in my life. There is nothing anybody said in court that suggested otherwise. *How can he just decide I'm crazy? How could I not have seen it coming?* "Counter allegations," that's what he'd said in his opening speech, and I knew then, only I talked myself out of it, because it made no sense. As if he'd made up his mind before ever hearing any evidence.

'Mummy! Move!' Lewis shouted. I was vaguely aware of a horn beeping. The lights had changed, and I hadn't noticed. *Keep your eyes and your mind on the road!*

Pulling into a service station with a Marks and Spencer attached, Lewis started to clap.

'I need to wee soooooo badly.' He had his car seat already open and jumped out the second I stopped the car. I quickly unbuckled Daniel, and we followed him into the shop to ask for the key.

Once Lewis had finished in the toilet, I grabbed a basket and flew around the shop at lightning speed, filling it with food. Anything. I just needed to get out of the shop. The checkout assistant barely looked up as she served me, chatting to her friend at the other side of the counter. Carrying a couple of carrier bags full of goodness knows what, I left the shop, with the boys running along to keep up with me. My head hurt, and my mouth was dry. Turning the ignition on we set off on the last part of our journey.

Back on the road, the boys munched on apples, and I focused on trying to see, as sheets of rain began to fall. "*I find that the father did not perpetrate physical, emotional or sexual abuse…*" The words rang in my ears. I wanted to scream.

How could he find that? I brought him doctor's evidence and teacher's evidence and drug samples. *"I find that the Mother caused the boys to ingest drugs…"* Obviously, that's what Madford was hoping for but how? I felt conflicted if I gave them Calpol! I'd had natural child births! We only ate organically (when we weren't running from the courts). It didn't make sense. This was a nightmare. How had this happened? None of it made sense. *"I find the mother to be wholly unreliable…"* But on what basis? The only people calling me so were those I was accusing of heinous crimes. Nobody else. The police had failed in their duty. That made them unreliable, not me. And the CPS had decided not to prosecute when the drug findings, alone, were proof my sons had been victims of a crime. But I was the unreliable one? This was one big sick joke.

I barely remember fleeing the court room. I could hear my heart pounding and feel my legs weakening, and I knew if I didn't leave, I'd collapse. Standing in the corridor, I caught my breath and looked around. A few lawyer types were milling in and out of various courts and a security guard was leaning against the stair railings. I'd planned to take a few minutes and go back, but like an epiphany, I realised that wasn't the answer. It didn't matter what the judge said. I had to protect my boys from their father, and there was, now, only one certain way to do that.

'We're here!' Lewis tossed his new iPad to the side.

'Yay!' Daniel enthused.

Returning to the Lodge we'd stayed in at Christmas was like a holiday for the boys. I told them it was a treat for us all because I'd been away so much recently.

'I can't wait to use the hot tub.' Daniel jumped up and down with excitement as I unloaded the car.

'Quick, get inside both of you,' I whispered. The boys looked at me, puzzled. They knew it was out of character

189

for me to be this stressed. 'Come on, don't let anyone see us.' I hurried them in.

Daniel bounced on the bed, and Lewis gathered all the bathroom soaps into a pile and placed them in the drawer of the locker beside the bedroom door.

'This is my locker,' he explained to us both, 'and if you want fancy soap, you'll have to come to me.'

I gave him a smile, but my eyes must have betrayed me.

'What's wrong, Mummy? 'Lewis asked, his face clouding over with concern.

'Nothing,' I lied. 'A last-minute holiday with my two favourite boys! Does life get better?'

I breathed a sigh of relief as soon as I closed the door to the lodge. I unpacked our bags as the boys explored the kitchen and living room. I had a dozen underpants each, but only a few t-shirts and trousers and one jumper, between them. It was hardly surprising. Once I'd made up my mind we were going, I knew we had to go quickly. My suitcase didn't fare much better as I pulled out a few formal blouses and a pair of ripped jeans I used for painting. *None of this matters,* I told myself. *We're together and we're safe. No-one will ever look for us here.*

***

Of course, they did look for us there, and they found us, and the rest, as they say, is history. They took my boys and gave full custody to the tyrant I'd sworn to protect them from. They considered charging me for kidnapping my own children but decided against it. I think they were afraid it might stir up more publicity. By taking the boys and running, I had inadvertently forced them to reveal a dirty family court secret – *children are taken from good mothers who allege abuse and placed in the care of alleged abusers* – and to make that truth palpable, they cloak it in lies. *The mothers are the abusers. The allegations are the abuse.* Once the boys were in the care of the state, the cover up began. The court released a statement to the press. In it, they named and shamed me and accused me of drugging my own children. Simultaneously, they shut down my right of reply by barring me from speaking about either child, making their version the only publicly available version.

Everything in retrospect is obvious, and it is now very obvious to me that you can trust no arm of the state. Not the police. Not social services. Not the CPS nor the courts. Not the media. We pay lip service to the idea of having learned lessons, from the horror of Jimmy Saville through to the corruption and ineptitude of Rochdale, but we have learned nothing. #metoo taught us to believe victims, it made us understand that people didn't make this stuff up, it made us see how widespread and endemic sexual abuse is, but, in the end, it taught us nothing.

I thought my boys would be listened to with compassion and an open mind. I thought the police would act swiftly and decisively. I thought they would seek out new evidence, instead of disregarding existing proofs. I thought the doctors were supposed to be looking for warning signs not ignoring them. I thought the guardian would speak for them, not put words in all our mouths. I thought the family court would keep our family together, not rip it apart at the seams. I thought, if I told the truth and prayed, God and the law would protect us.

But just like that, I have gone from being a full-time loving mum to a cardboard cut-out of a cliché, the woman scorned. And just like that, the epicentre of my universe, my two beautiful boys, have been taken from their home and world.

Eleven

I wake up with the same churning feeling in my stomach as I have done for the past one thousand, two hundred and forty-nine days. *Is this real? Has it all been a bad dream? When will it end?* Pulling my duvet over my head, I wrap my arms around the teddy that I sleep with, since the boys were stolen. I can't stay here alone with my thoughts and the ache in my stomach. Taking a deep breath, I check the time. It's 7:35am. Flinging the duvet back and climbing out of bed, I shiver. The weather is turning, and autumn is almost here. Another season gone.

Grabbing my dressing gown, I go downstairs to make myself a cup of tea and take it back to bed, opening my bedroom curtains to let in some light. I check the news with my mobile. It's habitual. One day, I will be reading that my ex-husband had been arrested. *One day soon…*

I check my social media pages. Someone could come forward any day. Another victim of his. *Any day now…* I scroll through my feed. It's just the usual messages of support and encouragement. They keep me going. A lady has written to tell me I'm her hero. This happens regularly.

I think so many people identify with my story because they, too, have lost loved ones to this heartless, defunct system. In me, they see a defiant fighter, and they envy my strength. "When my daughter was taken by her dad, it broke me completely," the lady's message continues, "but you seem so strong…"

If there is one thing I've learned through this personal perdition, it's that appearances can be deceptive. I am the face of my own campaign, and I take that responsibility very seriously. I know that if I present in a certain way, I will maximise public interest in my boys' welfare. But to suggest I am not broken is to know nothing of my pain. I don't show the world my tears or my terror. I don't make videos of myself in the dead of night when I wake from a dream where my boys are calling me and I am running towards them, screaming their names. At first in my sleep, and then into the stillness of my empty home. My empty life.

Sipping my tea and picking up the Bible from my bedside table I read my favourite verses in Isaiah 61.

The Spirit of the Lord God *is* upon Me,
Because the Lord has anointed Me
To preach good tidings to the poor;
He has sent Me to heal the broken-hearted,
To proclaim liberty to the captives,
And the opening of the prison to *those who are* bound;
To proclaim the acceptable year of the Lord,
And the day of vengeance of our God;
To comfort all who mourn,
To console those who mourn in Zion,
To give them beauty for ashes,
The oil of joy for mourning,
The garment of praise for the spirit of heaviness;
That they may be called trees of righteousness,

The planting of the Lord, that He may be glorified.

It always comforts me. After the reading I fall to my knees and pray,

'Thank you, Father, for protecting Lewis and Daniel, for rescuing them, for giving them strength. Thank you for exposing Damian Madford. Bring my babies back today, Lord, please.'

I think Lewis and Daniel might be the most prayed for children in the country. So many people praying for the safe return of my precious boys. I found Jesus shortly after the boys' disclosed, almost six years ago. Six long years. I wasn't exactly what you'd call religious, until that point. But once I heard those horror-filled words coming from the mouths of my babes, I knew that evil existed. And the only way to turn was God. A couple of years later, I started taking the boys to church. I would sit in Sunday school with them, after praise. I haven't been back to that church again since my boys were taken. Too many memories.

I finish the rest of my hot tea. I would need to get up. I had lots to do; I had to finish the book. The book, I felt strongly, would be an integral part of getting my sons home. The book had been God's answer to my prayer. Prayers and action. I couldn't just sit back, pray and do nothing. We had to listen and then take action. I had always thought the book would come after the boys had come back. But God had different plans, and I came to understand that I needed to write a book *now*. I get ready, have breakfast and sit at my desk. I open my laptop and click onto the chapter I was working on. I would do a couple of hours on my book. Not long to go now, there was an end in sight. I feel a rush of excitement that lasts for a second, before disappearing.

Looking outside the window I see the branches of the trees swaying in the breeze. The rain started to come on, and the tapping on the windowsill mirrored the tapping on my keyboard. The words were flowing. Sometimes, it felt as if I was in a trance, but my fingers continued typing as I traced the outline of our damaged lives for the whole world to see. It may seem inconceivable, even to me, now, but I am a private person. I have never sought attention or courted the limelight. I created this public persona to be the voice my boys were robbed of, to tell the story they told me and the police and the courts. Reading over the paragraphs I've just typed, I'm happy with what I have written. *This is going to be exposed. God has a plan.*

***

I need to do the food shop. The fridge is completely empty now. I can't put it off any longer. I can't face a fourth day of porridge for every single meal. Even by my subsistence standards it was becoming bleak. Checking the time, I see it's midday. There wouldn't be any school age children in the shops. I panic when I see children. The heart wrenching feeling when I hear a baby cry or a small child crying for their mummy. Especially when I see boys playing together, especially boys my sons' ages. I've been known to abandon my food trolley mid shop and just run. I barely ever leave the house these days, but needs must. I add a few essentials to the list I've prepared and mentally plan the food route. *I'll rush in and out, avoid eye contact, keep my head down, maybe pretend to be on my phone if someone approaches. I'll park straight outside. I can be there and home in under half an hour if I stay focused.*

Unloading the bags, I'm proud of my haul. I've bought enough food and toiletries to last a few weeks. I've taken to buying everything long life, the perfect food for a childless mother. I shove a half dozen tins of soup in the cupboard and remember a former life when I always had a pan of homemade soup on the go. The boys loved my soup. Cooking and eating together was one of our favourite things.

I saw them on a pre-recorded video last week. We get three video exchanges a year now. Once every four months, I get to sit in a room, supervised by strangers, and watch my children growing up on a tv screen.

Lewis is thirteen now. A teenager. I imagine he is about my height, maybe even taller. I flashback to a night in August, last year, when I woke up to the sound of crying. I knew it was Lewis. It was straight after he had been told the terrible news – the court had ruled that we couldn't have any contact for four years.

I see a deterioration in him, every video since, a lack of joy and of hope that he had, somehow, previously managed to keep going. The small glimmer of belief had all but disappeared. I whisper to him, *'Not long now Lewis, not long, you're coming home.'*

Daniel still has a baby face but has grown so much in three and a half years. My baby was going to be ten years old in a few months. *Please, God, bring them back before my baby is ten.* My perfect children. Trapped with their father. Tears well up in my eyes. How must the boys feel, when they see someone who looks like me, what about when friends at school ask them… "Why haven't you got a mum?" "Where is she?" "Is she in prison?" "Your mum drugged you, I saw it on the internet. Your mum drugged you! Your mum drugged you!"

Falling to my knees I ask Jesus to protect them and to keep them safe and to not let others bully them or confuse them or rob them of our precious memories.

My night-time routine is much like the morning, and as I sink into my mattress, my teddy by my side, I do a last scroll of my newsfeed and messages. One of these nights, I'm going to read how they've arrested Damian Madford and charged him. I sigh, tonight isn't that night. *All it takes, is one person,* I tell myself, *one other victim, one wife who knows, one mother who can't live with it any longer, one confidant who is weary from the burden of their knowledge and ready to tell the truth.*

And I know that someone will come forward. It's only a matter of time. And when they do, I'll get my sons back. It's only a matter of time. Rereading my favourite Bible passage, I feel the words of my God give me solace. Bending my knees for a final prayer.

'Thank you, Father, for protecting Lewis and Daniel, for rescuing them, for giving them strength. Thank you for exposing Damian Madford. Bring my babies back tomorrow, Lord, please.'

Thank you for reading
Everything is Going to Be Okay.

If you have enjoyed this book,
please head over to Amazon
and leave a review!

About the Author

Mum.

Acknowledgements:

To my amazing mum for her endless encouragement, drive and passion, my wonderful sister Leonie, for her dedication, energy and brilliant mind, my brother-in-law for his encouragement and support, my friends for always being there. And my eternal gratitude to a good friend; she can only be described as a 'God-send'.

Further Information

Sex abuse statistics

We can never know the true extent of people who were sexually abused as children, as well as the number of children who are being sexually abused right now. The numbers are far higher than present government predictions that state one in six boys and one in five girls have been sexually abused. The reason why these figures can only be estimated is that many people never speak to another person about their abuse. It takes on average five years for a female to speak out and a staggering twenty-seven years for males to speak out.

Prevention and early detection of abuse

The best way of protecting your child against any form of abuse is to talk to them from a very young age about it. You also need to familiarise yourself with the signs to look out for that a child is being abused as most won't speak out about it.

The majority of people wouldn't know what signs indicate that their child is being sexually abused. 'It wouldn't happen to my child,' we tell ourselves. 'They're only ever with family who look after them, so I don't need to educate myself,' and 'My child would tell me if someone abused them.' What about if that child is being constantly threatened with "if you tell anyone then you'll never see Mummy again…"? "If you tell anyone then you'll never see your family and your pets ever again…"

"Mummy will go to a country far away if you tell anyone…" "I'll kill your brother if you tell anyone…"

Most of us don't want to imagine that the person that we married is capable of inflicting such horrors onto their own child. That is why it is key to know the signs before it is too late. Then, if you carry out surveillance to find out if someone close is abusing your child and you obtain evidence on camera, you have all the evidence you'll need to keep the child abuser away from your child and hopefully secure a conviction.

Some of the emotional/behavioural signs that your child is being abused:

- Fear around a certain person/people, fear of being left with a person. If your child screams, shouts, cries and gets extremely distressed about being alone with a person, even if it is their parent, then something is wrong.
- Sleep problems – nightmares, bedwetting. If your child suddenly wakes up in the night with nightmares and insists on sleeping in your bed, then this can be a sign that they are being abused. Bedwetting can also be an indicator.
- Difficulty concentrating, poor performance at school. This can be a big sign. If your child is not making any progress and cannot concentrate.
- Dissociation. If you cannot 'get through' to your child, if they distract themselves with toys, not making eye contact, etc, going off into their own world.
- Depression, anxiety, anger, a lack of joy. Children's natural state is to be joyous. If they rarely laugh, get very angry over 'nothing' and are depressed, this is

a huge indicator that something is wrong.

- PTSD – this can look like ADHD.
- Crying frequently for no apparent reason, easily startled
- Suicidal thoughts
- Self-harm
- ADHD type symptoms
- Feelings of shame and guilt
- Difficulty coping with stress
- Separation anxiety, won't leave the side of the safe parent, won't let you out of their sight. It gets worse and not better. It should not be happening and should be something a small child gradually grows out of.
- Eating, appetite problems. Eating disorders.
- Sexualised behaviour – masturbation, acting out sexually with siblings. Children who haven't been abused would not naturally act out sexually with their siblings.
- Very disturbing episodes of behaviour that the child has no memory of afterwards (can be a sign of severe trauma or the effects of being administered with date rape drugs)

Some possible physical signs that your child is being sexually and physically abused:

- Soreness, itchiness, discomfort in their genital area and anus.
- Drowsiness after spending time with a person
- Clicking jaw – sign of oral rape
- Unexplained bruising
- Facial tic – a sign of distress

- Diseases on the buttocks/anus, localised in genital areas, UTIs
- Loss of control of bowels, when way past potty training age and no other explanation for it such as diarrhoea
- Frequent Headaches, stomach aches
- Child reporting that they 'wee'd out of their bum' after spending time with a person – this could be semen after being raped.

Side effects of date rape drugs:
Zolpidem:
- headaches
- drowsiness
- dizziness
- diarrhoea
- dry mouth
- chest pain
- palpitations (fast, strong, or irregular heart rate, or feeling like your heart is skipping a beat)
- grogginess

Benzodiazepines:
- drowsiness
- light-headedness
- confusion
- unsteadiness
- dizziness
- slurred speech
- muscle weakness
- memory problems

Most children who've been sexual abused were abused by someone they know. This could be a family member, a friend or someone who has targeted them, like a teacher or sports coach.

What if your partner is a paedophile?

Many of us wouldn't even entertain the likelihood of the other parent being capable of sexually abusing their child. It wouldn't even register as a possibility. People who sexually abuse their own children are surely very rare, aren't they? They'd be strange and easy to spot and you'd get a bad vibe from them...right? Wrong!

Our pre-conceptions of paedophiles can often be a far cry from the stark reality. They are not the deviant weirdos hanging around in rain-coats. They are living amongst us, sleeping in the same bed, lending us an ear when we need support. The huge majority of child sex abuse is perpetrated by someone close to the child, such as a relative or close family friend. Those statistics are undeniable.

It is the most insidious of crimes, the most horrific of crimes and yet one of the most difficult to spot. The fact of the matter is that symptoms of sexual abuse in children can often be mistaken for other things. Parents can often be 'in a spin' trying to find out what is wrong with their child but looking in all the wrong places. Many of us have who have had perfect childhoods would not recognise the signs of abuse. Most of the symptoms are behavioural and emotional and not physical.

If you're reading this list and recognising some of these symptoms in your child, you need to something. To not act could be potentially fatal. At the very least, you could spend a lifetime living in regret and despair when it's too late. Even the usual body safety talks won't make any difference in some cases where the abuser threatens the child into silence, with threats to kill the other parent/parents/pets etc.

What can you do?

1. The most important thing by far is to carry out surveillance (voice recorders, or a hidden spy camera). These devices are easy to find on the internet and very discreet. Keep copies should you discover that your child is being abused. Keep extra copies as well as giving one to the police, in case of corruption.

2. Encourage your child to have a close relationship with their teacher/teaching assistant. Teach your child to tell their teacher if they have any problems or are worried about anything.

Satanic Ritual Abuse – SRA

There are no official estimates of the number of people who have been ritually abused. Whenever people try to speak out about it, they are frequently not believed and discredited. Many are terrified to speak out as the cults who have abused and tortured them, have threatened them with death or the death of a loved one, if they do.

Characteristics of SRA

What we do hear, time and time again, from different survivors, is that SRA is generally carried out by a large number of people in a "coven". These people are from all walks of life and comprise both men and women. The children they abuse are generally their own children and family members, as well as a number of children who have been abducted such as the children who go missing each year from the "care" system. Unregistered births are another source of children, whom the system cannot track, who are believed to be among the victims of SRA. Repeatedly we hear survivors describing the same horrific practices, such as abortions, murders, and torture. These abusers don't stand out in any way. They are often upstanding members of society, raising money for charities, or running them and being active in community causes. They are spread across the class spectrum and count working class and elites among their numbers.

SRA does exist, and it is much more prevalent than we could ever realise. Satanist abusers have been positioned in certain roles, within the media, where they are in a position to debunk any claims of SRA and discredit anyone who speaks out about it. Many groups immediately jump on any claims of SRA, saying that they are false, and that the person is delusional. Why is there such motivation to cover up satanic ritual abuse? Well, the masses are slowly waking up. As SRA investigator, Wilfred Wong, says, there isn't a "conspiracy amongst toddlers around the world" all saying the same thing, describing the same horrors. Whether it is a religion or a belief system, the practices remain constant.

Some of the characteristics of satanic ritual abuse:

- Sexual abuse, by family members and their associates.
- Locking children in cages
- 'Waterboarding', near drowning
- Forcing the child/victim to ingest urine, blood and faeces
- Mind control
- Underground tunnels
- Placing children into coffins underground for long periods of time
- Physical abuse

- Torture and sacrifice of animals
- Torture and sacrifice of humans
- Eating the sacrificial victim
- Abortions
- Killing of babies
- Dressed in robes and masks

Satanic Ritual Abuse deniers

There are a large number of people who discredit, attack and mock anyone who speaks out about the existence of satanic ritual abuse. We have to ask ourselves why? Why do they go the extra mile to do this and to push the dangerous construct of 'false memory syndrome'?

Proof that Satanic Ritual Abuse (SRA) is real

When satanic ritual abusers are convicted, the newspapers tend to cover up the satanic ritual abuse aspects and instead focus on the sexual abuse elements. However, there have been a number of cases whereby the satanic ritual elements have been exposed.

There have been ten successful prosecutions where the evidence of SRA was openly examined during the trials. Given the very high standard of evidence required in Britain's criminal courts in order to secure a conviction, Beyond Reasonable Doubt, it is conclusive proof that SRA exists in the UK. The figure is not necessarily exhaustive, there may be some other successfully prosecuted SRA cases in the UK that have not yet been added to it.

Successful prosecutions are not the only evidence that satanic ritual abuse occurs in Britain. There are also numerous testimonies by SRA victims from all across the UK. Many of them continue to come forward with harrowing and graphic accounts of the abuse they suffered. The pattern of victims speaking up is on the increase, in spite of continued attempts by the establishment and media to "sweep SRA under the carpet" and pretend that it does not exist in this country.

List of successfully prosecuted SRA cases in the UK

1. On 9th November 1982, Malcolm and Susan Smith and Albert and Carole Hickman were convicted in Telford, Shropshire for a series of sexual and physical assaults against children, during the course of satanic rituals. Malcolm Smith carved an inverted cross on one child's abdomen and branded her genitals with a red-hot altar knife.

2. On 23rd July 1987, Brian Williams was convicted at London's Central Criminal Court for the sexual abuse of 15 girls and boys. He assaulted his victims on an altar dedicated to Satan and forced them to abuse each other. The rituals were performed with a Satanist pentagram drawn on the floor in blood.

3. On 8 August 1990, Reginald Harris was convicted at Worcester Crown Court after admitting to two specimen charges of unlawful sexual intercourse with a fifteen-year-old girl and her younger sister.
    Harris told his victims he was a Satanist high priest. The children were terrified into submission by Harris's Satanist rituals. He had drawn up a Satanist "coven contract of marriage" to the older girl.

4. On 3rd July 1992 a 57-year-old Satanist was sentenced at Liverpool Crown Court to twelve years in prison for

sexually abusing his niece. He had raped his victim two or three times per week between the ages of ten and twelve. The Court also heard details of a "black magic room" where the abuser kept an altar and ritual equipment. When the child was twelve, she became pregnant and was required by her uncle to give birth in that room. The victim was terrified by her uncle's satanic rituals. He threatened to rape her younger sister and kill her pets if she ever spoke of the abuse. On one occasion he snapped the neck of one of her pets in front of her and drowned another. Judge Dennis Clark told the man: "Your fascination with the occult or devil-worship played a part in impelling you towards this evil behaviour."

5. On 11th March, 2011, Colin Batley, the leader of a Satanist coven, was convicted at Swansea Crown Court of more than twenty sexual offences against children including eleven rapes. He, and other Satanists, had ritually abused children in Kidwelly, Wales, where their coven was based. The children, some as young as eleven, were subjected to "organised and systematic" abuse by Batley, his wife and two women coven members. Jacqueline Marling, 42, was jailed for twelve years for aiding and abetting rape, causing prostitution, indecency with a child and inciting a child to engage in sexual activity. Batley's wife Elaine, 47, was jailed for eight years on three charges of indecency with a child and sexual activity with a child. Shelly Millar, 35, was jailed for five years for indecency with a child and inciting a child to engage in sex. A fifth defendant, Vincent Barden, 70, admitted assaulting an under-age girl.

6. Two members of a witches' coven in St. Ives, Cornwall, were convicted at Truro Crown Court in December 2012 for their "ritualistic, sickening" sex abuse of young girls.

Jailing Jack Kemp for fourteen years and Peter Petrauske for eighteen, Judge Graham Cottle told them: "The offences range from the extremely serious to the truly horrifying." The judge said that the scars left on the victims were so obvious "that it would seem extremely unlikely that either of them have any real prospect of recovery." Petrauske was convicted of rape, aiding and abetting an attempted rape, and indecent assault. Kemp was convicted of ten sexual offences.

7. On February 9, 1989, Winchester Crown Court sentenced a sixty-year-old engineer to twelve years' imprisonment on two charges of incest with one of his five daughters. The man, who was described in court as a practising Satanist had fathered several children by his own daughter. To one of them, to whom he was both father and grandfather, he later committed acts of gross indecency and indecent assault. He made his daughter pregnant no less than five times. She had two miscarriages, a still-birth and a normal child. Another was profoundly mentally and physically handicapped. He claimed to have been "instructed by the spirits" to have sex with his daughter. When police arrested the man at his home in Fareham near Portsmouth, they found a small room in the bungalow that he described as his "magic room". There were occult symbols on the floor and on the walls, and occult and witchcraft books. They also found a black priest's robe and an altar. On it were phials of oil used in sex rituals. He pleaded not guilty to charges of incest with his four other daughters.

8. On 25 July 1988, Hazel Paul, a 28-year-old mother of three, was jailed for five years at the Old Bailey. Paul was convicted of falsely imprisoning a fifteen-year-old girl and

inflicting on her grievous bodily harm during satanic rituals. She also hypnotised the girl and encouraged a male friend to sexually abuse her. The jury heard a fifteen-year-old boy describe how Paul had ordered him to cut and carve the girl during rituals. Two other defendants were convicted with Paul of the assaults. The jury heard, and accepted by convicting, the explicit details of Paul's satanic rituals.

9. In 1987, Andrew Newell was sentenced to seven years in prison for killing his best friend in what was regarded by the police as a Satanist ritual. Newell stabbed Philip Booth five times around the heart. A murder charge was later reduced to manslaughter. Books on the occult and occult symbols were found in his room, with the words Lucifer, Leviathan, Satan and Belial. Timothy Barnes, QC, told the court that Newell's record box had been used as a makeshift black magic altar It was covered with bloody fingerprints and a smear of Philip Booth's blood. "When police opened the box, they found a lot of material associated with the supernatural," he said, "including candles that had been lit and a white-handled knife."

10. Peter MacKenzie was sentenced at St. Albans Crown Court in August 1989 to fifteen years in prison for four rapes and seventeen other sexual assaults against thirteen juvenile girls. His victims were as young as six.

An accomplice, John Baxter-Taylor, pleaded guilty to one charge of indecent assault and was sentenced to fifteen months in prison. The court heard how MacKenzie told his victims he was 'Asmodeus', an historic satanic name principally associated with 19th century French Satanism and made them recite prayers dedicated to him. MacKenzie had sexual intercourse with girls aged six and seven by promising them magic powers. MacKenzie said they could become witches in his magic circle. He terrified his victims by warning them that unless they took part in the rituals and kept silent about the abuse they would die. All the children had to undergo counselling and psychiatric help, which was predicted to last for several years.

(List compiled by Tim Tate and Andrew Boyd)

Unfortunately, for every SRA case that is successfully prosecuted in Britain, there are many, many more that the police refuse to investigate. Sometimes, because of links between the police and Satanic abusers. Sometimes, the CPS or other prosecuting authority may refuse to prosecute, due to Satanist influences.

The tragic reality is that today, in the UK, people with the right connections and influence are getting away with the most horrific form of child abuse, namely, Satanist Ritual Abuse. The general failure to investigate and prosecute SRA cases profoundly undermines the welfare of Britain's children and the Rule of Law.

A few facts about family court and the police

- Family court fail to take disclosures by children to their parents and family with any seriousness. In fact, they will often turn it against them;
- Police only charge a small number of sex offenders (1 in 25);
- Family court have a track record of placing children into the care of the parents who abused them.
- Family court often ban any contact whatsoever with the safe parent, as a means of punishing them.
- Family court ignore solid evidence and will accuse the safe parent of the very crime that the other parent has committed, leaving the children in a

desperate situation.

Parental Alienation counter claim (from leadership council)

Richard A. Gardner, M.D., is the creator of the creator and main proponent of Parental Alienation Syndrome (PAS) theory. Prior to his suicide, Gardner was an unpaid part-time clinical professor of child psychiatry at the College of Physicians and Surgeons at Columbia University. He made his money mainly as a forensic expert.

PAS was developed by Dr Richard Gardner in 1985 based on his personal observations and work as an expert witness, often on behalf of fathers accused of molesting their children. Gardner asserted that PAS is very common and he saw manifestations of this syndrome in over 90% of the custody conflicts he evaluated, even when abuse allegations are not raised. Gardner claimed that PAS is "a disorder of children, arising almost exclusively in child-custody disputes, in which one parent (usually the mother) programs the child to hate the other parent (usually the father)".

Gardner 's theory of PAS has had a profound effect on how the court systems in our country handle allegations of child sexual abuse, especially during divorce. Gardner has authored more than two hundred and fifty books and articles with advice directed towards mental health professionals, the legal community, divorcing adults and their children. Gardner 's private publishing company, Creative Therapeutics, published his many books, cassettes, and videotapes. Information available on Gardner's website indicates that he has been certified to testify as an expert in approximately four hundred cases, both criminal and civil, in more than twenty states. Gardner 's work continues to serve as a basis for decisions affecting the welfare of children in courtrooms across the nation. He is considered a leading authority in family courts and has even been described as the "guru" of child custody evaluations.

Because Gardner 's PAS theory is based on his clinical observations--not scientific data--it must be understood in the context of his extreme views concerning women, paedophilia and child sexual abuse.

Gardner on paedophilia

"There is a bit of paedophilia in every one of us."

Gardner, R.A. (1991). Sex Abuse Hysteria: Salem Witch Trials Revisited. Cresskill, NJ: Creative Therapeutics. (p. 118)

"Paedophilia has been considered the norm by the vast majority of individuals in the history of the world."

Gardner, R.A. (1992). True and False Accusations of Child Sex Abuse. Cresskill, NJ: Creative Therapeutics. (p. 592-3)

Similarly, "intrafamilial paedophilia (that is, incest) is widespread and ... is probably an ancient tradition"

Gardner, R.A. (1991). Sex Abuse Hysteria: Salem Witch Trials Revisited. Cresskill, NJ: Creative Therapeutics. (p. 119)

"It is because our society overreacts to it [paedophilia] that children suffer."

Gardner, R.A. (1992). True and False Accusations of Child Sex Abuse. Cresskill, NJ: Creative Therapeutics. (pp. 594-5)

In addition, Gardner proposes that many different types of human sexual behaviour, including paedophilia, sexual sadism, necrophilia (sex with corpses), zoophilia (sex with animals), coprophilia (sex involving defecation), can be seen as having species survival value and thus do "not warrant being excluded from the list of the `so-called natural forms of human sexual behaviour."

If you suspect a child or children are being abused, please act before the family court gets their hands on them and hands them back into the care of their abuser or their abuser's family.

It is important never to ignore your gut instinct, if someone feels a bit odd, not right, then it probably isn't.

Printed in Great Britain
by Amazon